MW00877848

The Line Between

by Kelsie Nygren
The Young Writers Series

The Line Between
Copyright © 2007 by The Benchmark Group LLC
ALL RIGHTS RESERVED

Published by:
The Benchmark Group LLC
148 Del Crest Drive Suite One
Nashville, TN 37217-4640
BenchmarkGroup1@aol.com

The integrity of the upright will guide them. Proverbs 11:3a

in association with:
McDougal Publishing
P.O. Box 3595
Hagerstown, MD 21742-3595
www.mcdougalpublishing.com

ISBN 978-1-58158-109-6

Printed in the United States of America
For Worldwide Distribution

Contents

Dedication 5

Acknowledgements 6

Rodd in Seattle 7

Pick a Jo, any Joe 15

Insanity and Phone Calls 21

Up and Away 27

Family Matters 37

Mr. Peterson, I Presume? 45

Working it Out 49

Mind over Matter 55

Enter Comatose 63

Rude Awakening 75

To Reach August 83

Somebody by my Side 89

Safe Haven 97

Nathanial's Story 107

From Ian with Love 117

In Sayta Clutches 123

Upon Gray Stones 135

New Powers 143

Out of Court 155

Closing Curtain 169

For my dad, who will always be my rock and my champion, and for my mom, my hero, who made me believe I could do this.

Kelsie

Acknowledgements

Just as there isn't one character in a book, there isn't one person who writes it. Without the people in my life, this might have remained just a dream. First and foremost, I thank my Lord Jesus Christ—for without Him, nothing could be done. My parents have been my constant support through all of this; I can't imagine this book without them. My Nana encouraged and inspired my imagination when I was a child, which started me on the path I now tread. I'd also like to thank Georgeann especially for listening to my rants and babbling, and always being there to work things through with me. Thanks to everyone at school for the constant support and love. And, last but not least, I'd like to thank the two women who made this all possible: Ms. Patti (Hummel) and Ms. Vicki (Huffman). So, thanks, everyone. This isn't just my book; it's yours, too.

Kelsie Nygren

ONE

Rodd in Seattle

It was raining.

Of course, it was often raining in Seattle, especially in the spring.

I sat at my kitchen table, watching dark splatters on my once-clean apartment windows. I sighed, knowing the windows probably would never be sparkling and decided to concentrate on what I had to do today. Never being able to master the complexities of a PDA, I glanced at my "To Do" calendar hanging on the wall. March 12, 2007—it hit me like a punch in the gut. That day was burned in my mind. One year ago today my friend and colleague, Emily, was murdered. At her memorial service, our boss, Gerald Dyose, said she was martyred for our cause. The logical part of my brain knew that sacrifices had to be made when fighting evil, but my heart cried out, "Why did she have to die?"

Pushing the sorrow into the back of my mind, a glance at the clock showed I was already running late. I dug my old, battered sneakers out from under the bed and shoved them onto my feet. Checking in the mirror, I saw that my blue hoodie was slightly wrinkled, as were my blue jeans. I tried vainly to stop wisps of chin-length sandy brown hair from forming a halo around my head. *My poor hair will never get used to this humidity*. My eyes, one brown and one blue, looked slightly sleepy. In other words, everything was normal.

"Well," I murmured. "This is as good as it gets. Better get going before Dyose blows his top."

I grabbed my keys and locked the door behind me. Slinging my raincoat around my shoulders, I ran down three flights of stairs. I was just about out the door when my landlady screeched, "Josephine Whitwalker! Get back in here!"

Already getting yelled at—this was promising to be a great day. "Yes, Mrs. Opal?" I asked, trying to look as pleasant as possible despite her angry face.

Penelope Opal was tall with brown hair pulled into a messy bun and dark eyes flashing with irritation—at me. She reminded me of my boss. Their life's mission and utmost pleasure seemed to be yelling at me. "Don't 'Yes, Mrs. Opal?' me, girl."

I tried hard not to roll my eyes. At twenty-three, I was hardly a "girl."

"Your rent is long overdue," she scolded. "Yesterday you said that you'd get it to me today. Well, it's today right now. I want my money."

I groaned. Naturally, I had forgotten all about the rent, as I did on a regular basis. "I'll be getting my paycheck today," I said hurriedly, noting her look of growing rage. "I'll get it to you this afternoon."

Opal's frown intensified. "You can't keep doing this, Whitwalker," she snapped. "One more time and you're out."

"Thank you!" I said, darting out the door.

"I'd better see a check in my hand before midnight!" she yelled at my rapidly retreating back.

I waved over my shoulder to show I'd heard her. I didn't want to get her any angrier than she already was. This was my third apartment in two years. The problem wasn't just my forgetfulness. My job didn't pay enough. I argued repeatedly with my superiors that, for all the life and limb stunts I did, I deserved a larger paycheck. Don't get me wrong, I'm not money-obsessed or anything; it's just a necessity of life. I do my job because I love it. But you'd think being a Rytra would pay more, wouldn't you?

A Rytra, after all, is a person who can control the elements of Light. Elements are in everything: from the air you breathe, to the water you drink, to the sun and moon. The elements are separated into two divisions, Light and Dark. The elements of Light consist of air, water, and, of course, light. The elements of Dark are earth, fire, and darkness.

There are those who can control Dark, too. They are the Sayta, and they are humanity's mortal enemy. Light and Dark can never be around each other without repelling. So it is with Sayta and Rytra. We are destined to fight each other until the end.

Both Rytra and Sayta came into being eons ago. From what I've read in our history books, we Rytra were created to fight the Sayta who are totally evil. It's not like Rytra get a lot of credit from those we are defending because the general population doesn't know about us. A gene is missing in those who are not Rytra or Sayta. That missing part of their DNA allows our activities to go undetected. We are just normal human beings as far as they are concerned.

The control of the elements itself is simple. All Rytra can sense the elements constantly. We are born with this power, but we don't normally realize we can control the elements while we are children. When we reach our teens, the awareness becomes more insistent. That nagging feeling in the back of the mind leads to many a paranoid teenager. We can fully appreciate and control our powers only after we are trained. We feel the elements after that, like a soft sensation tickling the edge of our consciousness. If we only reach out slightly, deepen that bond, we can take control of the elements.

There are repercussions to exercising our powers. Exhaustion is the usual result, although I've heard of extreme cases where the elements annihilated the person.

All around the world, Rytra have formed an organization to hunt Sayta. We call ourselves RODD or the Rytra Organization to Defeat Darkness. I work with other Rytra in Seattle. So here I stood, my mind wandering and soaking wet because I had stupidly forgotten my umbrella, waiting for the 7:55 a.m. bus to take me to headquarters. It was ten minutes late, which ensured my boss would be furious. I ran the last three blocks to the five-story building that housed RODD. The outside was a mustard color with peeling paint, deliberately giving no hint of what it housed. Once inside, I rapidly walked down the hallway, hoping that Dyose wouldn't notice me coming in more than fifteen minutes late. Again.

"Whitwalker!"

Apparently, no such luck. Aw, well. I'd never been very lucky anyway.

"Get in my office before I haul you in here!"

Judging from his voice, I guessed he was in a really bad mood. I edged towards his office, earning more than one sympathetic glance. Everyone feared Dyose and pitied anyone who irritated him. Today, it was me. I poked my head in his door slowly. Dyose was sitting at his desk, chewing a cigar savagely. He was partially bald and not very happy about it, had muddy brown eyes and a large frame. His nose lay almost flat against his face. As soon as I stepped in, his head shot up and those eyes locked onto mine. Watching him like a wary animal, I sat down in one of the hard chairs.

"How are you doing, Mr. Dyose?" I asked amiably, hoping to appease him.

"How am I doing?" he bellowed. "Do you realize what time it is? I would be a lot happier if you managed to arrive on time for once in your life."

I smiled weakly. "I'll make a note of it."

He twitched but managed to restrain his natural reaction to strangle me. "Is there anything else, sir?" I inquired, ardently hoping that there was not.

"As a matter of fact, there is," he said. "I have a job for you, Whitwalker."

I brightened considerably. I had not had a job in quite a while and was looking forward to it. Anything to help the cause, after all. The Sayta had been getting sneakier, hiding their powers more carefully. Lately, every time a tracker got a lock on one of them, the Sayta fled the scene covering the trail with intense darkness.

Dyose must have noticed my look, "Don't get so excited, Whitwalker." He pushed a file in front of me with a photo attached. He was scruffy looking with a half-grown beard and deep-set eyes. "His name is Joe Year. He has been keeping low until lately. Have you noticed how many buildings have burned in the last month? All the work of this man right here." He tapped the picture with one pudgy finger. "I want you to go and do your thing. Report to Nathanial Vene. He's the tracker who just transferred in from Mexico. And no taking unnecessary risks; you're one of our best and can't be replaced." This last was said grudgingly, but I beamed at the compliment.

"Thank you very much, sir." I paused for a second, wondering if I dared go on. Remembering Mrs. Opal's wrath, I did, "Excuse me, sir, but since I am one of the best, don't you think I deserve a raise…?"

Dyose didn't look up from his paperwork. "We'll see after this job. Now, get out of my sight before I suspend you for impudence."

Amazed that he hadn't shot down my idea of a raise immediately, I decided to find this new partner, Nathanial Vene, after getting a quick cup of coffee—not decaf. We Rytra always work in teams. There's the fighter, which is me, and the tracker, which in this case would be Mr. Vene. The tracker finds the Sayta and the fighter actually attacks. Dangerous? Yes. Did I love it? Definitely.

"Hey, Jo," a friendly voice said as I walked into the break room.

I looked up and smiled. Ian McKinley was one of the kindest people at RODD, a terrific tracker, and my best friend. He was tall, red-headed, and gray-eyed. Today he had dressed in green and yellow—he liked to be noticed. Originally from Dublin he had come to Seattle a few years ago and was recruited to RODD. He was unaware of his powers at the time, which was extremely unusual. I was one of his student instructors, teaching him how to control his powers on a basic level and learning alongside him on other matters.

"Hey, Ian, I finally got a job."

His eyes sparkled. A job was of interest to any Rytra: tracker, fighter, or paper pusher. "Really? Who?"

"A guy named Joe Year."

His laugh lines crinkled. "Jo is going to hunt Joe. Now that is just weird."

I smirked. Ian was like that. He took boyish amusement in most things and never seemed to be gloomy, although he did have a fierce temper when riled. Many said he was a bright candle in the darkness. I had to agree.

The break room door opened. A man with raven black hair, deep blue eyes, and appearing to be a bit over six feet walked in. He was a few years older than me, perhaps around 27. He wore a loose black shirt and black jeans with black boots. I got the feeling he liked black. I had never seen him before.

"Josephine Whitwalker?" he asked, eyes fierce and bright. "I'm Nathanial Vene."

TWO

Pick a Jo, any Joe

The next thing I knew, I was following this man down the hallway that led to the Jeeps in the garage. He was silent except to ask me if I knew what I had to do. I replied in the affirmative, which apparently was the key word for his off button. I tried several times to come up with a subject to talk about, but he gave clipped, short answers.

When we claimed a Jeep, Nathanial opened the door for me. I was slightly surprised but covered it up quickly. It's a sad thing that the world has been reduced to men who generally know nothing of chivalric values. We women don't expect them to and then are surprised when they're the least bit gentlemanly. I bowed my head slightly in thanks and got in.

"Do you always talk this much?" he asked as he started up the engine.

I grinned. "Ya know, a lot of people seem to complain about that."

"I wonder why."

I was delighted by the man's humorous, sarcastic tone. Most Rytra are too serious and full of themselves to have fun. It could get to be a dreadful bore sometimes. Nathanial steered the Jeep up the garage ramp, and out onto the rain-drenched streets. "So," I said, "where is Mr. Year hiding?" Friendliness was gone, replaced by professionalism.

"Supposedly in his house on 12th Street. I can't press too

hard on him. Then he'd notice us, and we'd have to chase him all over the city. Right now he's stationary."

I dug into my pocket, searching for the small treats hidden there. Triumphant, I pulled out two red and white wrapped candies. "Walnetto?" I offered.

For the first time since I had met him, Nathanial seemed slightly taken back. "What?" he asked, glancing at me.

I chuckled and said in a mock-scolding voice, "What? Have you never heard of Walnettos before?" I took his silence as a no. "Well, it's pretty much just caramel with walnuts. I always have one before a job. Call it a good luck charm. So, do you want one?" For the barest second, a twinge of sadness shot through me. Emily's silvery laugh sounded in my mind, but I pushed it away, not willing to bring up painful memories.

"No, thank you." His voice had gone back to cool politeness. I sighed. I always hated working with a new partner; I much preferred working with Ian. He was already working on something, so I was on my own with this new guy.

I was beginning to get nervous, anticipation making my adrenaline soar. You would think that after nearly six years of fighting the Sayta, I would get used to it. Some considered them the worst of all evil. They were to be destroyed, no matter what. I didn't totally agree with that philosophy. Maybe some part of my innocence remained with the thought that they, too, deserved a chance to live. Then one would commit some horrendous crime, and my resolve would harden once more. I was a Rytra, opposed to the Sayta. No matter what, I will fight them, as I have for years.

We slowed to a crawl as we neared 12th Street. I closed my eyes, separating myself from the physical world as I prepared to summon Light. This wasn't a necessary process, but it took less energy than just summoning the elements outright. In doing this, I had to put my whole trust in Nathanial, a person I hadn't even known an hour. While I was in this state, anyone could harm me and I wouldn't be able to stop them. I would literally be dwelling more in the elements than my own body.

Once I was firmly within the boundaries of my power, I opened my eyes and looked at my surroundings. The Jeep had come to a complete stop before an ordinary red brick house. The neighborhood was normal; the person in that house was not. First things first, however, I had to set up a barrier. I glanced at Nathanial, who nodded grimly. Joe Year was in there, maybe even waiting for us.

Taking a deep breath, I concentrated on summoning the element of air. It responded to my silent call, coming up to form the requested barrier all around the house and the Jeep. The air solidified into a shield that would protect us against an attack. Once it was up, no one could get inside and no one could leave unless the barrier was broken. It was possible for a Sayta to break the barrier from sheer force of attack, but highly unlikely. I was experienced and very good at what I did. The downside of having barriers was that it took a constant stream of energy to keep them up. I had become strong enough to keep them up for a while without much conscious thought, but it certainly wasn't my favorite activity. Keeping them up too long could immobilize you when you let them down, so it was always good to be wary of the time.

I carefully got out of the Jeep, leaving Nathanial. He wouldn't be coming in with me. If worse came to worse, he had enough power to get me out of here, but I sincerely hoped that wouldn't happen. His job was to watch for other Sayta.

A certain fear gripped me as I walked to the house, but it

was a kind of fear that I knew well. The door opened with a soft squeak at my push.

As I carefully entered the house with an extra barrier around my person, I could feel the darkness. I wasn't a tracker and couldn't actually pinpoint the Sayta, but I could feel them when they were near. They were so permeated with Dark, just as Rytra were with Light, that it was impossible not to feel them.

Some Rytra couldn't stand being this close to the Dark. One of the reasons I was so good at my job was that I was better than most at withstanding the Dark. But it always made me faintly nauseated.

The house had a single lamp flickering in the foyer. Rain made the windows black with only an occasional lightning flash illuminating the room. I edged into the living room, light dancing around my fingertips. The furniture looked expensive and, on the edges, slightly singed. This one specialized in fire, for sure.

There was a noise to my left. I spun quickly. A man stood before me, hands at his sides and wavering slightly. He looked anemic; his face and skin a deathly pale shade, his black eyes devoid of any spark. His hair, thin despite his young age, hung limply around his shoulders. He looked at me without any expression, hands twitching slightly. I didn't move, waiting for the blow I knew was going to come. Although he might be weak, Joe Year would fight. They always did.

He moved surprisingly fast. Before I knew what was happening, a fire ball hurtled towards me. I concentrated on keeping my shield up. The fire hit the air barrier around me and dissolved into embers. I retaliated quickly, not giving Year a chance to strike again. There was a sharp cry of pain as the light hit the man squarely in the chest, knocking him back a few steps. "Are you crazy?" I blurted out. "Who in their right mind wouldn't put up a shield?"

He looked at me, lips twitching into a cruel smile. "I haven't been in my right mind for a long time," he growled. There was a hint of maniacal laughter in his words. Then, without further ado, he leapt at me.

I was not prepared for this. My shield had been constructed to keep elements out, not actual human contact. It took too much power to keep both away. I gasped in pain as his claw-like hands scrabbled at my face. I fended off most of the blows, but his sharp fingernails dug two gouges in my cheek. Hot blood dripped down my face.

Rytra fighters trained several times a week, and I was certainly no weakling. I managed to throw the thin man off me onto the floor. Not hesitating, I struck, the power of light streaming from my outstretched hand. The blinding whiteness overwhelmed the man, covering him completely. But right before it did, I thought I saw something on his face. I thought I saw … no. Never mind. A trick of the light, that's all. He didn't even have time to scream, which was better on the whole. The screams of death always echoed in my mind long after.

Only when I was sure he was dead did I let up on the steady stream of light. Crouching beside him, I gently closed his eyelids. There was not a mark on him, and for possibly the first time in his life, his face was peaceful. When the police arrived all they would see was a person who had been taken by a heart attack before his time. I let out a shaky breath. With the death of the Sayta, the worst of the Dark had already fled the house, but my job wasn't over yet.

In the kitchen, I rifled through drawers until I found an

address book. I stuffed it into my pocket. In a bedroom thirty minutes later I found another address book in the fake bottom of a dresser drawer. There were more numbers here. Most were probably dead ends. Still, as a professional, I never pass up information.

Besides the books, there was little of value. Nathanial was leaning against the car, tapping his foot, when I came out. I walked toward him, dispelling all shields as I did. Only when the pressure to keep the barriers up was gone did I realize exactly how tired I was. I stumbled a little down the sidewalk but managed to get to the car. Nathanial grabbed my arm and helped me into the Jeep. His grip was powerful.

"Everything okay?" he asked as he climbed into the driver's side. He didn't sound particularly concerned, but he did cast a quick glance in my direction.

I smiled weakly, resting my head against the seat. "I'm alive aren't I?"

He snorted as he looked at the scratches down my face. "Okay then, next question. How in the world did you manage to get hurt with a barrier up?"

I winced. "He attacked me physically," I said shortly. "But do you know what the funny thing was?" I murmured, staring at the ceiling of the Jeep. Without waiting for a reply, I said, "He didn't put up a barrier around himself."

"But that's suicidal," protested Nathanial.

I nodded. "I know. It's …." I paused, trying to gather my thoughts together and get the words out. "It's almost as if he *wanted* to die. And right before he did … I thought I saw him *smiling*."

THREE

Insanity and Phone Calls

"That's crazy!"

All I wanted to do was go home and sleep, but before I could, I had to report to Dyose. I was in his office at that moment being ridiculed. "I know it is, sir," I replied, sinking lower in the chair. "But that's how it seemed."

"No Sayta would commit suicide!" Dyose said stubbornly for the umpteenth time. "Their instinct is to keep fighting, no matter what!"

I exchanged glances with Nathanial, who was in the torture room with me. "I understand your concern, sir ..." I started to say.

"It is not concern, Whitwalker. It is disbelief!" yelled my boss.

"May I go now?" I whined. "I've told you everything I know, and I'm exhausted." Besides, if you don't believe me after I've told you everything a dozen times, I don't think I'll be able to do anything more. That last bit, I kept to myself.

"NO!"

"Dyose," Nathanial suddenly said in a commanding tone. I blinked and stared at my new partner. "What is it you want?"

Dyose's left eye twitched. "To uncover all the details,

Vene," he growled. "We might have a situation on our hands. I need to know everything."

"Is it really necessary to keep Miss Whitwalker here? She's told you all she can."

"Yes," I agreed. "She's told you all she can." *Okay, this is strange*, I thought. *Why is he taking my side? Well, I'm sure not gonna contradict him.*

"Fine," Dyose grumbled. "Leave, Whitwalker." I was halfway to the door before he finished. "But you and Ian go through those address books and start making calls. He finished his assignment, so he's all yours."

I sighed. Waving agreement over my shoulder, I left the office to find Ian. But he found me first. "So, is it true?" he nearly shouted. "Did you really have an insane Sayta on your hands?"

I led him into a conference room and closed the door. "Well," I replied, "that's what everyone thinks."

Ian's eyes were bright. "Are you saying that you disagree?"

I heaved myself up on a table and tried to explain. "He admitted that he was insane, and he sure was acting like it."

"Then what's the problem?"

I ran a hand through my hair. "I don't know. It just doesn't seem right to me. Never in our history has a Sayta or Rytra gone insane. So why now?"

Ian winked. "You know what they say. There's a first time for everything."

I glared at him. Ian laughed, plopping down into a chair with the phone. "So, what are we supposed to do?"

I showed him the two address books. "Start with the one from the fake drawer."

A few hours of calling produced little progress. Most of the numbers were people who didn't know the truth about Year. Ian asked questions that only a Sayta (or a Rytra) would understand, and no one did. Around 3:00 p.m., Nathanial walked in. I was lying on the table on my back, staring at the oh-so fascinating ceiling.

"I brought you something to eat," Nathaniel said, handing me wrapped burritos from the vending machine.

I grabbed one hungrily and took a bite. Once I had swallowed, I gave him my most charming smile. "First you stand up for me with Dyose and now you feed me? I think I've fallen in love."

Nathanial blinked, unsure what to make of this. Ian gave him a friendly slap on the back. "Don't take her seriously. She's harmless, really," he said in a thick brogue.

I rolled my eyes. "What's with the brogue, Ian?"

Ian's face fell. "I was trying to impress one of RODD's best trackers with my Irish heritage."

"And why would that impress anyone?" I asked slowly. I had to say something to cover my surprise. Nathanial, one of the best trackers? That was a tidbit of information I hadn't known. I put two and two together. *If Vene is one of the best trackers, and I'm one of the best warriors, Dyose must have been really nervous about Year. Why don't they tell me this stuff before I go into the field?*

"If you two are finished, we should get back to work," said Nathanial with a hint of irritation in his voice.

Ian and I exchanged looks. "We?" the two of us said in unison.

Nathanial grimaced. "I have been assigned to work with you two in determining whether Joe Year was or was not sane."

He obviously thought such work was beneath him. Well, if that was his attitude, it was time to bring him back to earth. I chuckled silently. This should be fun...

I got another phone and put Nathanial to work. He and Ian divided up the remaining list and started calling. I listened on the headset, slowly chewing a candy bar, until Ian's frantic signaling made me stop in mid-chew.

"Well, Mr. Year," said a cold male voice. "We haven't heard from you lately."

"Yes," said Ian, trying his best to sound like Joe Year. "I've had a bad virus."

"Ah. Get to the point. Why did you call?"

"I was wondering what to do next," said Ian carefully, glancing at me. I nodded. It seemed to be the safest course.

There was a hiss of irritation over the line. "Can you get any more thick-headed, Year? We need that stone. The other factor we can get later. Find it for me, Year. Your head is on the block."

We all exchanged glances, the same question in our eyes: What stone?

"I'll need more details about the stone," Ian quickly said.

There was silence on the other end of the line, then a slow chuckle. "Very good. I applaud your attempt, Rytra." Without another word, the line went dead.

"Did you manage to get a lock on the location?" Nathanial demanded.

I checked the computer and felt my eyes go wide. The whole screen was completely black. Even from this distance, I could feel the evil seeping through it. I jumped to my feet, ran to the monitor, and placed my hands on it, ignoring the sharp pains shooting through me. It was dangerous to touch the Dark-infested computer, but there was always the chance that the Light would travel completely through it and back to the original source, purging and destroying the sender. I managed to purge the Sayta darkness from spreading, but unfortunately, nothing was left on the computer.

I backed away, waving my hands in the air as if they were burned. "You idiot," said Nathanial and Ian in unison. They each grabbed an elbow and pushed me into a chair. The pain was subsiding, but the touch of Dark was like poison to Rytra.

"It's okay," I said, watching as the Dark slowly receded. "I'm fine."

"You should know better," they said, once again at the same time. My two partners looked at each other in surprise. I was just about to comment on how alike they were when Dyose burst through the door, making me nearly jump out of my seat.

"What's up, boss man?" Ian asked.

Dyose sent him a slightly annoyed look. "You all are going to England."

We traded looks, and I asked the obvious question. "Why?"

"I just got a call from the head of RODD in London—Scott Peterson. He's been getting some strange reports of the Sayta over there. Seems like they're going … mad."

A horrible silence ensued, as if our tongues were as numb as the rest of our bodies. Then I broke the spell and stood.

"Looks like we're going to England then."

FOUR

Up and Away

Beepbeepbeepbeepbeepbe—crash!

I buried my head under the covers. Why had I set the alarm so early? The sun wasn't even up. I glanced in irritation at the broken pink clock on the floor and rolled onto my stomach. I was almost asleep when the doorbell rang. "Go away!" I yelled.

For one blessed moment, it seemed that they might go away. Then I heard pounding on my bedroom door. "Jo!" yelled Ian. "Get up, lazy bones!"

I blinked. What was he doing here? In a rush it all came back to me. The plane to England was leaving today. Hours upon hours of flying. I shuddered. My fear of flying had been with me since childhood. But it was an unavoidable evil. Mumbling, I got tangled in the covers trying to get out of bed and tripped. I yelled and heard Ian laughing. "Fell out of bed again, eh?" he called through the door.

"Ah, just shut it!" I replied. I was not a morning person.

"Are you ready to go?"

I opened the door after throwing on a robe. Nathanial was admiring a nearby painting, paying no attention to our conversation. "Do I look ready to go?" I snapped. "How did you get in? The door was locked."

Ian smirked. "Well you see, dear Jo, a long time ago, you told me that a certain magical key to unlocking the mystical door into the Land of Unwashed Pots and Pans and General Messiness was under the mat. So I, the great warrior and hero with magical key in hand, dared to enter the Land of Unwashed Pots and Pans and General Messiness, at danger to my own being, of course. But that's what a hero ..."

I slammed the door in his face. "If you're hungry, there's cereal!" I yelled.

I pulled off the fuzzy blue and white pajamas that my mother had given me for my last birthday. My thoughts wandered to my mother. She was a real nut about the beauty and history of England, so my family moved there when I was ten years old. I moved back to the United States to join the RODD forces because I always remained loyal to America. Because I had lived in England for years, I knew what the weather was like. I pulled on a red sweatshirt, blue jeans with sequins on the pockets, tennis shoes, and a worn red baseball cap. Grabbing my suitcase that I had—with some foresight—packed last night, I darted out of the bedroom.

Ian and Nathanial were sitting at my kitchen table waiting impatiently. Actually Ian was eating and Nathanial was reading my morning paper. "Well, let's go already!" I said as if I'd been the one kept waiting. They glared at me all the way down the stairs.

Before we could reach the front door, Mrs. Opal blocked the way. I skidded to a halt, which made Ian bump into me and Nathanial bump into him. "Oopsie," I said. Silently, however, I was yelling at myself: I hadn't picked up my paycheck at the office.

"Where's the rent, Whitwalker?" my landlady roared.

"Well…" I cleared my throat. "You see… I kind of… um… forgot?"

Opal's left eyebrow twitched. "Then you're on notice— I'm putting your apartment back up for lease."

I winced, but there wasn't anything I could say. I didn't have the money. "Guess I'm looking for a new home when we get back," I said as cheerfully as I could once we were in the parking lot.

Ian eyed me sternly. "You're going to go through all of the apartments in Seattle if you keep this up."

I walloped him in the stomach. He bent over double, wheezing and laughing. "Joking, joking!" he said once he had gotten his breath back.

"Now, now, children, play nice," Nathanial said as he climbed into the driver's side of the Jeep.

"Hey!" Ian and I protested.

Nathanial rolled his eyes.

I sat in the back behind the passenger seat. Once we were off towards Tacoma International Airport, conversation died. The traffic was bad (as usual), and Nathanial seemed very glad when we arrived at the airport. I, on the other hand, began to feel fear gnawing at my insides. I looked nervously at the planes waiting to take off. Still, a girl has to do what a girl has to do.

The plane was delayed, so we sat in the boarding area for an hour and a half longer. I figured it was either a malfunction easily fixed or something that needed to be double-checked. Neither of these options made me feel any safer. By the time we boarded, we were all irritable and past ready to leave. Well, I didn't want to leave, but I wanted to see what was happening in England as well as see my family. Oh, the conundrum! Our seats were halfway back. Ian immediately claimed the window seat. Because I didn't want to sit next to the aisle, I sat in the middle.

The "Fasten Your Seatbelts" sign starting flashing. The plane backed away from the gate and moved down the runway. As the wheels left the ground, I closed my eyes tightly and gripped the armrests with all my strength. Well, technically, it was one armrest and Ian's hand. I could feel his eyes on me but didn't look at him. He squeezed it reassuringly. Only when the plane had straightened and was flying smoothly did I open my eyes and let go of Ian's hand.

"Man, you have a strong grip when you're scared," Ian said, massaging his purple and white hand.

I laughed nervously.

"I take it you don't like flying?" Nathanial asked.

"You think," I grumbled bad-temperedly. It was one thing for Ian to know my fears. But for this man, whom I barely knew, to know I was afraid of flying, well, I wasn't pleased. It wouldn't do for the world to know that Josephine Whitwalker, Rytra Extraordinaire, was a chicken when it came to planes.

Ian, as he always did when flying, went to sleep. Soon his soft snores filled the row. I gave him a few good-natured pokes, but he slept right through them.

"You seem to be close to Ian," Nathanial said after a while.

"Uh, I guess," I glanced at Nathaniel askance. "He's my best friend."

Nathanial looked out the window as he asked in an odd tone, "Is that all?"

I was highly offended by his prodding. "Hey, Bucko, back off. What's it to you anyway?" In case you haven't noticed, I get testy when I fly. Still, my personal life was mine alone. It didn't matter if I had feelings for Ian or not—it was the fact that a person I barely knew was asking me about something private.

Nathanial shrugged. "Sorry. But, since we are going into enemy territory, I think I have a right to know whether or not the relationship between the two of you might interfere with our mission."

I was still angry but also confused. "What do you mean by that?"

"I don't want personal disagreements to make us easy fodder for the Sayta."

I snorted. "Like that would ever happen. Hey, listen. Ian and I are professionals; we have been partners for a year and have never had any problems carrying out our assignments successfully. Your insinuations are insulting."

Nathanial shrugged again. "Whatever you say, Miss Whitwalker."

Muttering under my breath, I took a deep breath and decided to follow Ian's example. Closing my eyes, I drifted off to sleep. Only it wasn't a restful sleep. My memories had come to haunt my dreams once more.

****

I was still young; 19 to be exact. I didn't know many people at RODD, outside of my trainer George, and my boss Dyose. Ian wasn't there yet. But I did have one friend, someone more like a sister.

Although Emily was my age, she looked about 16. She had dark red hair falling to her waist, brilliantly blue eyes, and a scattering of freckles across her nose. She was barely five feet, one inch— smaller than me—and I was usually the shortest person around. She wasn't afraid of anything; even in serious situations, she would smile. Her laugh, like silvery bells on a silent winter's night, always warmed the heart. She had a stutter but wasn't embarrassed by it. She said it was part of her. Emily was a beautiful innocent girl but, in the end, she understood things far better than I did.

It was a sunny day when it happened. Emily and I were on foot searching the streets for one Rich Kline. He was a Sayta, of course. Why else would we be looking for him? He wasn't that powerful— or so everyone thought. A tracker had a lock on him, and Emily and I, both fighters, were pursuing him. I had a phone earpiece, listening to the tracker give us directions. It was supposed to be a routine job. No one expected it to turn out the way it did.

"Jo," said Emily, turning to me with sparkling eyes, "w-when we're d-done, s-shall we go out f-for lunch? A n-new Italian p-place just opened."

I grinned. "Sounds good." By this time, both of us were used to the killing. We didn't like it, but found that eating lunch or doing something normal afterwards helped.

"Walnetto?" I offered.

Emily grinned, taking the piece of candy and popping it into her mouth. She chewed for a moment, then nodded as if deciding something.

"Y-you know, it s-s-should be a-a tradition!" she exclaimed.

"Hmm?"

"Before e-every job, y-you s-should have a W-walnetto."

I laughed. "That's a good idea, Em. But you'll have to do it with me."

Emily winked. "O-of course. We're partners."

"All right," said the tracker in my ear, bringing me back to the job, "he went into an alley on your left. It's the perfect place for an ambush. Be careful."

"Aren't we always?" I said, starting down the alley.

The crackle of static was my only response.

The alley was long and dark, the looming roofs of buildings on either side shielding it from the sun. At the end, a high wall blocked any escape. Emily and I walked down the alley warily. To my left, Emily's breathing quickened a little. She was a bit claustrophobic. "Don't worry, Em," I whispered to her, barely able to hear my own voice. "We'll be out of here in no time."

She nodded, albeit shakily.

"You sure about that?"

Before we could turn to the voice in the shadows, absolute darkness filled the alley. I yelled, searching blindly for Emily. Calling to the light, I bade it to lift the darkness. It did, flooding the scene. After my eyes adjusted, they immediately went to my side. I froze in horror, unable to move, yet wishing with all my heart that I could.

A scream.

Blood. It was everywhere. Emily, eyes wide, one hand over her chest where the red flower was growing, slipped to her knees. Above her stood the man we were supposed to hunt, Rich Kline. He had long, greasy blonde hair and brown eyes that were disturbingly calm. In one hand he held an elemental-made knife of Dark. Wrought of earth, fire, and darkness, it was so powerful there was little that could guard against it.

"Noooooo!" My heart seemed to scream out for revenge.

My hand flew up, light streaming from it. The strands of light wrapped around Kline, strangling him, killing him. He hacked at the light with the elemental-made knife, but the strands held, fueled by anger, sadness, and loss. Nothing could stop it.

The knife fell from his limp hand, hitting the ground, only to disappear a moment later. The light strands also disappeared, dropping the nearly unrecognizable body onto the ground. I didn't spare it a glance as I rushed to Emily.

I grabbed her limp body, gently lifting her head onto my lap. Emily stared up at me, her eyes calm and bright. The small smile that always graced her lips was there, peaceful and beautiful. I was crying, shoulders shaking so hard I could barely concentrate to call forth the water—the healing water.

"No, Jo," Emily whispered. Blood stained her lips and trickled down her chin.

I gently wiped it away, struggling to make sense of what she said. "But, but you're dying!" I wailed, sobs wracking my body. Dying. No. It wasn't possible. It couldn't be possible...

Emily's eyes still didn't show any fear. "Yes," she said. "I am. And I don't think people should use the elements to change that. You know about my beliefs. When it's time for God to take us, we shouldn't be kept alive by our own powers."

"But it's not your time yet, Em," I sobbed softly. "It can't be."

She took one of my hands in hers. "It's all right, Jo. I'm not afraid."

"Emily…"

"Jo." Her eyes were shining brightly, as she stared at nothing. "Oh, Jo! The Light! It's so bright … so beautiful!" The smile never left her face as she closed her eyes and was escorted away.

It was only when I was back at RODD that I realized something. In her last moments, Emily hadn't stuttered once.

****

I woke up with a start, my heart beating painfully. As dear a friend as Ian was to me, Emily and I had been like sisters. We were family. I sighed. Despite the two men sitting with me, I felt terribly and utterly alone.

FIVE

Family Matters

We arrived in England at dusk; brilliant oranges and reds still colored the sky. Stretching, Ian looked around the airport. "Hey, Jo, is someone picking us up?"

I was waiting impatiently for the baggage to arrive on the merry-go-round. "What?" I asked absently.

"Is someone coming to get us?" he asked again.

"Aha!" I said triumphantly, spotting my bag. I grabbed it, tugging it out of the mass of suitcases. Nathanial helped me get the others until we had amassed all of our paraphernalia. By this time, however, Ian was slightly irritated.

"Jo!" he said impatiently.

"What?" I snapped.

"Is someone coming for us?" he said through gritted teeth.

I snorted. "Of course. Do you think I would leave us stranded at an airport? Try to not get so worked up about this stuff. You need to calm down, Ian."

He twitched and stalked over to the seats. Nathanial was smiling, but it didn't reach his eyes. Not for the first time, I wondered why he was so cold. It seemed as if he never allowed another's emotions to touch him. It made me sad. Part of me wanted to ask why he was like that, but my good sense refused to allow me to ask such inappropriate questions.

Judging from our conversation on the plane, he didn't hold to such common etiquette.

I realized suddenly that I was hungry. I hadn't felt like eating anything on the plane. I turned to Nathanial, "Hey, Vene, why don't you go get us something to eat?"

"Why me?" he asked bluntly.

I smiled sweetly. "Because Ian is sulking and I need to watch for my family."

He grumbled a bit more, but obediently went off. "So," I said, plopping down next to Ian, "what's the plan?"

He sighed, allowing his sulkiness to melt away. "Well, we need to learn some more of the situation first, of course. We'll go visit Peterson tomorrow."

I nodded, leaning back in the seat and stretching my legs out. "Hey, Ian?"

"Hmm?"

"Thanks."

He glanced at me. "For what?"

I shrugged slightly. "Just for being there," I said.

He ruffled my hair. "No prob," he said, his voice kind and warm.

My thoughts zoomed off to the conversation between myself and Nathanial on the plane. I glanced at Ian. He was handsome, but to me he was just Ian, my best friend. Stupid Vene. Why did he bring that up anyway? And why would he make such assumptions? I don't act differently towards Ian than I would any other friend. Do I?

"You look worried, Jo," said Ian. I jumped. He was looking at me with concern.

"I'm fine," I said. "Just thinking."

"About what?"

Suddenly all thoughts of Ian, Nathanial, and my feelings flew out of my head as I saw David. He was shorter than average, like me, and had light brown hair and nutmeg brown eyes. He was looking around for us. At least I had remembered to call him when our plane was late, so he hadn't been waiting very long. I jumped up, waving wildly to catch his attention. "Davy!" I shouted gleefully.

He turned and broke into a grin. "Hey, Jo!" he said happily. He ran and picked me up in a bone-crushing hug. "How are you doing?"

It had been more than a year since I had last seen my brother. "Not bad," I said happily, clinging to his arm. "And you?"

He laughed his familiar, jovial laugh. "Very good! My newest book just made the best-seller list."

"Really? That's great!"

Davy was a novelist who wrote historical fantasy and was currently involved in a long saga set at the dawn of time. He still attended college, being only 21, but his writing ability was already well known in the literary world. "How're Mum and Dad?" I asked. Without even realizing it, I had slipped slightly into my British accent. That usually happened when I visited England.

"Pretty good."

I grinned and leaned in a bit closer. "And how are things with Madeline?" Madeline was Davy's girlfriend. They had been going out for nearly a year.

He blushed slightly. "She's good too," he mumbled, looking down slightly.

I snickered. "I think someone's in looooooove."

"Shut up."

Turning around, I saw that Nathanial had returned with hot dogs. Tugging on Davy's arm, I dragged him over to meet my co-workers. "Davy, you already know Ian."

They shook hands. "Good to see you again," said my brother.

Ian nodded. "You, too. It's been a long time."

"And this is Nathanial Vene," I introduced.

They shook hands. I let Ian and Nathanial take care of the bags while Davy and I walked to the exit. "Two guys, sis?" Davy asked, one eyebrow raised.

I punched him playfully. "Not my fault," I pointed out. "And anyway, you know and like Ian."

"True," he conceded. "But the other guy?"

"Again, not my fault. Blame Dyose." After all, everything was always his fault.

We reached the car, a small red Peugeot 307. I groaned at the sight of it. "Haven't you gotten a new car yet, Davy? How will all the luggage fit?" I moaned.

"Obviously not easily," grunted Nathanial as he struggled to arrange baggage in the trunk—or boot—as we call it in England.

I looked at him expectantly. "And where, pray tell, is the food I sent you to get?"

There was a chorus of groans. I chuckled, climbing into the car happily. It was good to be home.

I must have fallen asleep because the next thing I knew Davy was shaking my shoulder. I stared blankly for a moment before realizing that the old Peugeot was outside my parents' house. All sleepiness forgotten, I bounded to the door and flung it open. The house looked exactly the same, with its off-white walls and English cottage decor. The clatter of pots and pans I heard could only mean one thing: Mum was cooking.

She was at the stove muttering to herself. Her graying brown hair was cut short, but a few strands of bangs still fell into her eyes. She wore an ankle-length, bright orange dress. The sight of her brought unexpected tears to my eyes, and it took a moment to banish them. When I had managed to do so, I called happily, "Hey, Mum! I'm home!"

She spun around, her expression a mixture of exasperation at me surprising her and joy at having me back. "Josephine Whitwalker! Don't surprise me like that!"

I grinned and hugged her tightly. She smelled like flour and spices, and I breathed in deeply. "I'm sorry," I whispered into her ear. She softened at my words, arms tightening around me.

"It's good to have you back," she said. She smiled, wiping away tears with a corner of her apron. "Now shoo. I need to finish this. Go say hello to your father."

A slight chill made its way down my spine, but I obeyed. My father was sitting in the living room watching television and not listening as Davy introduced Ian and Nathanial. I knelt by his side. He looked older than I remembered. "Hello, Dad," I said gently, making sure my words were clear. "How are you?"

The sixty-year-old man blinked at me. "Who are you?" he asked. Although I stayed outwardly calm, my heart was aching. My father had an advanced case of Alzheimer's and only occasionally recognized anyone now.

"It's me, Dad. Josephine."

Out of the corner of my eye, I saw Ian looking at me pityingly. Nathanial was studiously looking at his hands, but I knew he was listening. All of a sudden, I felt the old anger rise up in me. I hated people pitying me. I opened my mouth to say something, most likely something harsh, but Mum announced that dinner was ready.

I sat between my dad and Davy. Nathanial was across from me. Mum brought out her creation, which turned out to be chicken gumbo and fresh bread. I dug in eagerly, it being my favorite meal, and let Davy do the talking. The pleasant conversation we were having about Madeline was cut short by my father speaking.

"It's nice to see you again, Josephine," he said suddenly, eyes on me.

There was an uncomfortable lump in my throat. "You too, Dad," I said.

He looked blank for a second, then smiled and asked, "Do you remember the time we went fishing together at Lake Michigan?"

I winced, tried to conceal it, and failed. Forcing a smile I said, "Of course I do, Dad." My heart was thudding in that way that feels as if your chest is going to burst.

My father turned back to his food, and then looked up at me. "Who did you say you were again?" Without waiting for an answer, he turned to Davy, "And where is Madeline? I want to see my daughter."

A sudden rush of tears filled my eyes. He thought Madeline was his daughter? Why wouldn't he? After all, she was probably around more than I was these days.

There was a murmur from someone at the table. Raising my head, I stiffly forced a smile. "It's okay," I said, trying to sound as normal as possible and failing miserably. "Madeline is probably good for him."

Mum turned the conversation to another subject, much to my relief. Looking down, the food looked sickening. The walls of the room seemed to be closing in and I couldn't breathe. I left the table without a word. No one called me back or followed me.

The kitchen opened up onto a small porch. Half of it was under the roof, while the other half was open to the stars. I went there, as I always did when I was troubled or needed some time to myself. Leaning against the railing, I blew out my breath in a long, low sigh. The Alzheimer's was getting worse. It was hard to understand, harder to bear. I didn't want my Dad to think Madeline was his real daughter or that I was just someone he went fishing with. I wanted my real Dad back, but I knew that I would never see him again. He was lost in a darkness not entirely unfamiliar.

Closing my eyes, I rested my hot forehead against my shaking hands. I heard footsteps behind me but didn't turn around. For a long moment, the person didn't say anything. In a tone filled with either sadness or pity, Nathaniel said, "It must be hard."

To tell the truth, I was surprised that it was Nathanial. For some reason, it warmed my heart; even his pity didn't seem so horrible at that moment. Maybe he's not totally unfriendly after all.

I glanced at him, noticing the real sympathy in his eyes.

"Yeah," I murmured, unable to think of anything else.

He joined me at the railing. Together we silently watched the stars, looking out at the vast infinity of space and knowing that so much of life is out of our control. We must trust God—even in the dark.

SIX

Mr. Peterson, I Presume?

My parents had a large house, which meant I had my own room. Despite the privacy, my sleep was restless and filled with my father's words. By the time I rose, it felt as if I hadn't slept at all.

Nathanial and Mum were enjoying a cup of coffee when I entered the kitchen. I plopped into the seat next to Nathanial, rested my head on my hand, and closed my eyes.

"Tired, dear?" asked Mum kindly.

"You know I hate flying. Seeing Dad like that doesn't help either."

"Well, maybe some food will help."

I perked up a bit, even opening my eyes. "Bacon and sausage and pancakes?" I asked hopefully, giving her my best puppy dog look.

She patted my hand. "Anything you want, dear."

By the time it was cooked, Ian had joined us. We lingered over breakfast. None of us really wanted to leave this homey atmosphere and face the harsh realities of the world we knew too well. Eventually, with regretful sighs, Ian, Nathanial, and I started for the city.

Although the outside of RODD, London had plain white walls, the inside was different. It wasn't expensively furnished. The walls were green and the floor cheap tile, but brightly colored rugs, an assortment of paintings, and a few tapestries added life. Rytra of all sizes and races talked easily with one another. It had none of the strictly business feel of RODD, Seattle.

"Nice," I breathed appreciatively. "I wish our headquarters was like this."

"We do pride ourselves on our homey office," said a cheerful voice behind me.

I turned to a woman a good bit older than myself. She was large, round, and wearing the brightest pink blouse I had ever seen. Her brown-blonde hair was swept into a bun, and her golden-brown eyes sparkled with enthusiasm.

"I'm Amy. Are you Josephine Whitwalker?" she asked.

I smiled. "Yes I am. And this is Nathanial Vene and Ian McKinley, my two partners."

She surveyed our group for a moment. "Scotty's been waiting for you."

She led us down a hallway. Several people greeted us, and I got the feeling this RODD was usually a happy, relaxed place. But, despite the atmosphere, I could tell that people were tense and worried. That made me worried. No one else seemed to notice. We would be talking with Mr. Peterson soon. Maybe he would have answers for us.

Amy stopped in front of an office and bade us goodbye. I exchanged glances with the others, before knocking on the door.

"Come in."

The office was rather plain with only a few chairs, two filing cabinets, and a messy desk. Standing at the desk was a man about Nathaniel's age. He had a boyish look with curly blonde hair, freckles, and bright blue-gray eyes. He wore a white button-up shirt and jeans. He was about the same height as Ian, a little shorter than Nathanial.

"Mr. Peterson, I presume?" I said in a cheerful voice as I shook his hand.

"Scott Peterson, at your service, Miss Whitwalker," he said jovially.

His manner put me at ease. We quickly went through introductions and sat down.

Scott linked his fingers together and observed us over them. "I assume you know why we have called you here," he began with a more somber tone.

"Because the Sayta have been going insane?" I guessed, trying to keep my voice light yet not joking. I must have failed, judging from the look Nathanial sent me.

He nodded. "Yes. It is very strange. They're suicidal and attack recklessly, without any reason. From appearances, they are going mad. And if they are going insane, who is to say that the Rytra won't be next? On top of that, Rytra have been mysteriously disappearing."

I blinked. "That I did not know," I murmured. Louder, I asked, "Has there been any warning at all? Did they say anything before vanishing that would give us a clue?"

Scott shook his head. "No. One day they're here and the next we have no idea where they are." He lowered his voice slightly. "Although we have searched, we haven't found any trace of them. And the Sayta number seems to be rising."

"We've been having that problem in Seattle too," I scowled. "Nasty vermin."

"I couldn't agree with you more," Scott laughed but his smile faded quickly. "I don't suppose you have any leads?"

"The best we've got is something about a stone. Vene and I went off to fight Joe Year. We came away with a good phone number and listened to some freaky guy talk about a stone and 'the other factor.' But we have no idea what he meant."

Scott grinned. "I do like the way you phrase things, Miss Whitwalker." He shook his head slowly. "I'm afraid that we have heard nothing about a stone." He brightened suddenly. "But with you here, and Mr. Vene, I'm hopeful we will find some answers."

"And what am I, chopped liver?" Ian asked sulkily. He really hated being left out.

I smiled at him. "Of course not, Ian, dear! You're chopped leprechaun!"

He gave me a dirty look.

Scott stood. "Since you'll be here frequently, would you like a tour? And then maybe lunch to change the subject, at least for a little while?"

I agreed that a break from this topic would be a relief. Perhaps then the gnawing worry would leave my stomach. Scott showed us around the building telling about the accomplishments of RODD in England. I walked beside him, but all I thought about was how hard this assignment was going to be. Though with these people by my side, it would be manageable. Hopefully.

SEVEN

Working it Out

The next morning I woke to pounding on the door. "Jo!" yelled Ian. "Get up and dress! We're leaving."

I covered my head with the sheets. "Aw, Ian! I don't wanna!"

"Jo, sometimes you are the most immature person I have ever met," he snapped.

"Hey, at least I have a title," I replied. "What do you have? A bad Irish brogue?"

There was a chuckle. From inside the room. I poked my head out of the covers, and found myself looking into Nathanial's blue eyes. "How did you get in?" I screeched, walloping him over the head with my pillow.

He gently took the pillow. "Ian sent me in."

"Why didn't he come in himself?" I ran a hand through my hair trying to put it in some order. I was wearing a thick shirt and jogging pants, so I didn't care if Nathanial saw me. But it was the whole principle of the thing. Guys were not supposed to barge into a lady's room without knocking. Well, technically, Ian knocked, but he didn't get my say-so before sending someone in. "And since when do you take orders from Ian?"

Nathanial shrugged. "It's very amusing."

I stuck out my tongue. But I was rather pleased. *He's*

getting more human every day. Maybe he just needs to get to know someone before he opens up. I dove into my luggage and came up with a thick sweater thingy that went to about mid-thigh over blue jeans. I shoved Nathanial out before changing and was totally ready in five minutes.

"Hah!" I said triumphantly to Ian as I entered the kitchen. "I have another title. Fastest changer in world history!"

Ian rolled his eyes. He started to say something, but my enthusiastic greeting to Madeline—who apparently had come over early with homemade cinnamon buns—cut him off. "Thank you, thank you, Madeline!" I said fervently. I hugged her tightly.

She laughed and patted my back. "Good to see you too, Jo."

A few minutes later, stuffing the last bite of a delicious roll (okay, the third roll) into my mouth, I glared at the two as we got in the car. "Oh yeah!" I exclaimed about ten minutes into the drive. "Hey, guys, did you have any weird dreams last night?"

Nathanial glanced back at me, "No."

"Ditto. I take it you did?" said Ian.

"I had a freaky dream where a voice was telling me: 'Keep the balance between Dark and Light, Josephine. Fight for the right. Don't be afraid. You are the one that can withstand the Dark.' Then two guys were talking about some stone." That was a mini-version, but I didn't want to get into details.

"The stone the Sayta mentioned?" asked Nathanial sharply.

"Maybe. But I don't think the voice was a figment of my imagination."

Ian snorted. "What else could it be, Jo? Your subconscious controls your dreams. You were thinking about the stone and Sayta. And that whole withstanding the Dark part? You know you're able to handle that better than any of us."

"Maybe," I replied softly. But the more I thought about it, the more I believed something else was going on.

Ian and Nathanial were whisked off to do whatever trackers do as soon as we reached the RODD building. I was in the break room. Thankfully, Amy came in. "Hi, Jo," she said cheerfully.

I smiled. "Hullo, Amy. Is there anything I can do?"

Amy shook her head. "No. They never need you until the end. You know that."

"Yeah." We stood in silence for a minute. "So, what is your job, anyway, Amy?"

She smiled. "I direct people, dear. In emergencies, I'm a fighter. I can hold my own, although my own sometimes holds me." She patted her large stomach, laughing. "I'm good with the elements, but my girth prevents fast movement." She gave me a sidelong glance. "Of course, I'm nowhere near you."

I blushed. "I'm not that good."

Don't be modest; everyone knows you're one of the best in the world," Amy said. "If you're bored, we have a gym. I don't go in there myself, but I'll show you."

Rytra mainly use the elements for war, but it is always good to be physically fit, as fighting Joe Year had proved. I changed into workout clothes provided for employees in the women's locker room and entered the gym where three guys were working out. Most Rytra were men, so women were outnumbered, especially when it came to actually fighting. Ninety percent of women Rytra were trackers or directors.

I disregarded the stares of the men. What is it with men and their need to eyeball women? A girl doesn't like to be ogled; it makes her feel like a commodity. Once I warmed up, I ran on a treadmill, then started beating up a punching bag.

"Having fun, Miss Whitwalker?"

I jumped. Turning, I looked at Nathanial. "That's the second time in one day you've surprised me," I said. Grabbing a towel, I wiped sweat off my face. "And you can stop with the Miss Whitwalker business. My name is Jo. Two letters—shouldn't be hard to remember."

A flicker of a smile darted across his face. *Wow. He's even more handsome when he smiles.* Berating myself for thinking such a thing after getting angry earlier at men for the same thing, I pushed those thoughts away.

"If you insist that I call you Jo, then please call me Nathanial," he said smoothly.

I threw the towel in a bin. "All right. Shall we get some lunch, Nathanial?"

"Yes... after you take a shower."

I glared at him. "I feel so loved," I said. Ten minutes later, I found everyone gathered in the break room. I plopped into a seat next to Amy and helped myself to the fettuccini. "So, anything?" I asked with a mouth full of noodles.

"Don't talk with your mouth full," Ian said absently.

I ignored him and looked at Scott. The blonde man shrugged. "No, although for a minute we thought Nathanial had locked onto something. Unfortunately, he lost it."

"But we've already made progress," Amy gushed. "We should have a lock on someone by tomorrow."

Nathanial bowed his head slightly. "You put too much faith in me."

Amy waved one pudgy hand in the air. "Nonsense! Don't be modest, my dear Nathanial. Take credit where it's due."

Ian gave me a wry glance. "Why did I come again?" he asked softly. "With Nathanial here, they have no need for me."

I swatted him on the arm. "I'm sure you'll get your glory, my little leprechaun."

He nodded. "Hopefully, sooner rather than later."

I was in the locker room the next day, bored out of my wits. I had finished my workout and redressed when boredom was violently swept away.

The door burst open. Amy panting, shouted, "They... got a... lock... hurry, Jo... he's moving fast, and... he's very powerful."

"Where is he headed?" I asked, my voice calmer than I felt.

Amy's eyes were dark with fear. "He's heading for your mother's house."

Mind over Matter

I felt like my whole body had been dunked in ice water. The only thing I could feel was fear: the fear of finding them dead, of not getting there in time, the very fear of not knowing. If you didn't know, your imagination played a hundred different horrible scenarios in your head. All I could hear was the beating of my own heart in my ears—pounding, pounding, always pounding.

"Jo?"

I looked at Amy, took in a great big breath, and then darted off. I ran as fast as I could. Turning a corner, I collided with someone else running with a loud smack. My head had connected with the floor painfully. Then strong hands pulled me up. I looked through bleary eyes at Nathanial.

"Thank goodness!" I exclaimed, out of breath, more from fear than from running. "I was looking for you. We need to go!"

Nathanial's hands, which were still around my elbows, tightened for one brief moment. He grabbed my hand and tugged me down the hallway. I followed him for a moment, and then realized that we weren't heading towards the exit. I dug in my heels, bringing us to a stop. Before I could open my mouth to ask where we were going, he said peevishly, "It'll take too long to go by car. Scott and a few others are quite gifted in transportation."

I blanched. The one time I had tried a transportation, the air had dumped me in some unknown land, and it took hours for me to persuade the air to send me back.

I returned to the present, realizing that Nathanial was dragging me along. I thought about disengaging my hand. Then I realized that I didn't want him to let go of my hand. I was surprised by these strange feelings of sudden familiarity, but I pushed them away. Saving my family was much more important.

Just when I thought I wouldn't be able to keep my impatience reined in any longer, we came to a spacious empty room with bare white walls. In the middle of the room stood Ian, eyes closed. I had seen that look many times. I had guided him the first time. Ian had a pinpoint on someone, and he was determined not to lose it.

Scott looked up as we entered. His face was shadowed, and there was something in his eyes that I couldn't quite place. Fear? Uncertainty? Or even anger? Whatever it was, it was gone almost as soon as our eyes met. *It's like he's trying to hide something from me,* I thought. *But that's just truly ridiculous. He's our ally and a Rytra. Why would he try to hide something?*

"Are you sure about this?" I asked.

Scott gave me a frank look. "If you want to get there before the Sayta does, we don't have time for anything else," he said in a tense voice.

I could tell he was nervous. But nervous about what? Our safety? No, that couldn't be it. Looking at Scott, a sudden and unexpected uneasiness filled me. There was something different about him; I was sure of it. He wasn't like normal Rytra; somehow, he didn't belong here. A little

voice at the back of my mind said he was like… like a false
Rytra. Like that could ever happen! There were three kinds
of people in the world: those without powers, Rytra, and
Sayta. There was nothing in between.

"Ready?" whispered a voice in my ear.

I jumped. Turning to look at Nathanial, I realized that he
still clutched my hand. I gave his a little squeeze of consent
and nodded. I took one of Ian's hands and Nathanial took
the other. Then other Rytra gathered in a circle with their
hands linked. Closing their eyes, sweat appeared on their
foreheads as they commanded the air to transport us. A
breath of air brushed my cheek, sending a shiver down my
spine.

As the air worked its magic, the white walls faded away. I
looked at Ian and Nathanial, but they too were dissolving in
a barrage of wonderful colors. They were like chalk draw-
ings caught in a rainstorm, all the colors swirled together
until it was impossible to tell what the picture had been. I
took a deep breath, concentrating on the tangible feel of
their hands around mine.

Then, quite suddenly, that disappeared too.

Something's gone wrong, was my first thought. I looked
around, but there was nothing to see. Only darkness. In the
place between places, there was literally nothing. I was in a
void. It was not a nice feeling. Something had gone very
wrong.

I looked down at myself, but there was nothing to see.
After all, it wasn't my physical body that was traveling.
When I came to someplace tangible again, my body would
rejoin it. Although I was certain I should be panicking right
about now, all I felt was an icy calm. *Where were Ian and*

Nathanial? Were they here in the void with me? Or had they managed to make it out? Since I couldn't answer that question, I moved on to the next: *How in the world do I get out?*

Every problem always has a solution. My father used to say that, and it was my motto. "Mind over matter," he would say. "Apply yourself, Jo. All you have to do is think. You're a girl of action, but if you learn to think more, you'll find that your brain is your greatest power." He would always tap his head at this point, winking roguishly. "Mind over matter, my girl."

But your mind betrayed you in the end, I thought sadly.

For a few long moments, I sulked. *This is getting you nowhere. Think, Jo, think! What to do, what to do… think, think… wow, that sounded a lot like Pooh Bear. Can I get sidetracked easily or what! Back to the problem: how to get out of nothingness?*

I decided to try calling to the elements. Nothing. In the nothingness, nothing could answer because there was nothing. It was very confusing. I tried to remember if anyone had ever told me how to get out of nothingness. I couldn't recall anything, so I was on my own. *Jolly blooming perfect!*

Mind over matter.

That phrase again! But I'm not even matter. Right now, I'm not tangible. But… if I became tangible, I wouldn't be stuck here. Yes, that's a good solution, Jo dear. The only problem is that you don't know how to become tangible again!

Mind over matter, mind over matter! I paused. *Aw, man! My family!* I forced myself to calm down. *Stop it, Jo. Nathanial and Ian will take care of them.*

If I hadn't been in the nothingness, I would have blocked everything out. But, as there was nothing to block out, I simply concentrated on believing that I was tangible. I concentrated on what I felt like when I was real. The heaviness of my weight, the feeling of my hair brushing my neck, the material of my clothes against my skin; all those little things. And the next thing I knew, those things were real. I could feel gentle breaths of wind against my neck.

My eyes opened in shock. I was outside my parent's house with Ian and Nathanial next to me looking very bewildered. I let out my breath in a whoosh, sagging to my knees in sudden exhaustion.

The first thing I said was, "What went wrong with the transportation?" None of us had an answer. And we didn't have time to worry about it.

I ran up to my house. Flinging the door open, I yelled, "Mum, are you there?"

"In the kitchen, dear," came my mother's voice calm and chipper.

I let out a sigh of relief and slumped against the wall, running a hand through my hair absently. My mother came out of the kitchen. "Is something wrong?" she asked.

I gently grabbed her elbow. "Is anyone else home?" I asked as I led her to the back bedroom. My father was sitting in bed watching TV and didn't even look up.

"Only the two of us," replied my mother. "What's going on, Josephine?"

"Make sure no one leaves the house; I'll explain later. Don't worry. The boys and I have everything under control. Whatever you hear, don't come out."

Fear shone on her face. But instead of questioning me, she pressed her lips tightly together. "Be careful," I heard her whisper as I closed the door.

Ian was still maintaining a lock, eyes half-closed. Nathanial was standing still, eyes bright but calm. He gave me a small nod as I came out. Taking up my position between and slightly in front of them, I settled down to prepare a shield and wait.

After about fifteen minutes, Ian said in a hoarse voice, "He's coming."

I raised my hands slightly, palms inward. I was preparing myself for him to come at me in a rush, but the Sayta did nothing of the sort. He strolled down the street, hands in his pockets. He was an ordinary looking man with light brown hair. Despite his appearance, there was an air of Dark and power around him. He came right up to our gate before stopping. His eyes quickly flickered over us all. They paused on me and a slight smile curled his lips. Then he spoke.

"There really isn't need for a shield. Violence isn't my intention."

"Hah! No matter what you plan to do, I'm not letting it down," I spat out.

He smiled but said nothing. "May I come into the yard?" he asked, gesturing slightly. "It is very uncomfortable having to talk at this distance."

"Fine," I said shortly to the man. Once he was inside, I asked bluntly, "What do you want?"

"Why would you assume that I want something?"

I snorted.

He smiled again. "All right, Miss Whitwalker, we'll do it your way. Just give me the stone and I'll be on my way."

I scowled. "This is the second time I've heard someone mention a stone. What's the big deal with this rock?"

The man waggled his finger. "Ah-ah. Please, don't act

innocent. We know you have it, but it belongs to us." His eyes glinted dangerously. "And I suggest you just hand it over, before something very nasty indeed happens to you."

"I don't have a stone, and I don't know what you're talking about. Obviously you should have figured that out if you'd had any brains at all." It wasn't the best idea to anger a Sayta, but I was annoyed and upset.

The man flashed a feral smile, "Maybe you don't, but your companion does." He jerked his head toward Nathanial.

I turned to face him, keeping one wary eye on the man in black. "Nathanial?"

He was glaring. "I have no idea what he's talking about, Jo. Look out!"

I turned just in time to bring up the shield and deflect the man's darkness. I would never forget that face; devoid of humanity, intent on destroying us, he attacked.

Pushing back the darkness, I struck with light. He hissed in pain, flinging one hand over his face despite the shield protecting him, but I pressed on. Harder and harder, until he screamed and his barrier shattered. He staggered backwards, fell to his knees, then keeled over completely. As soon as he was down, I let up on the light and replaced it with air bonds to hold him. Nathanial was already by his side, checking for a pulse. "I think you've overdone it," he said. "He's going to need hospital treatment now."

I was leaning against Ian, panting. It had been an incredibly short fight, but intense. The previous adventures in nothingness had weakened me. "But he's still alive, right?" I gasped. To get to the bottom of whatever's going on, we need him alive.

Nathanial nodded. He grinned at me. For some strange reason, my heart began to beat rapidly at the sight of that grin. "I think Scott will be pleased," he said.

Later that night, I was sitting on the couch in the living room, staring at the phone. Why me? I picked up the phone and dialed the number. Don't pick up, don't pick up, I thought. Putting it off would not make it better, but it would give me temporary relief.

"Hello?"

Ugh. "Hello, Mr. Dyose? It's Jo."

He sounded annoyed. "Well, what are you waiting for? Report!"

I winced and did as I was told. "Well, sir, we just had a stroke of luck today. We captured a Sayta."

"And?"

"Well, he's sorta comatose at the moment…"

"Whitwalker, I swear…" I could hear the rage in his voice; he apparently wasn't happy with the health of our only prisoner.

I muttered, a bit defensively, "I had to. I couldn't let him walk away."

Dyose sighed. "Try not to let it happen again."

I winced at his sarcastic tone. "Yes, sir," I replied humbly. The phone went dead, and I gratefully hung up.

NINE

Enter Comatose

The hospital medicinal smell made me wrinkle my nose. It was just Scott and me today. Ian and Nathanial were at RODD headquarters, trying to track down another Sayta. Scott had insisted I come with him to the hospital to check on our comatose prisoner. I wasn't happy, because hospitals make me edgy. When I complained, Nathanial seemed surprised, but quickly turned almost... cruel.

"What?" he had said in a slightly sarcastic tone. "So, you're afraid of airplanes, telephones, and hospitals. Is there anything you aren't afraid of?"

I was stung by his words. Here I thought he was becoming more human, as we got to know each other better. Well, I suppose cruelty was a human trait. Usually, I enjoyed a little sarcasm, but I was hurt this time. "I'm not afraid of hospitals," I snapped. "I just don't like being there."

"Why?"

"Because all I can remember about hospitals is going there to visit Dad when he was sick, and then Davy when he nearly died from a car crash," I said slowly.

An abashed look flickered over his face. "Oh. Sorry."

"Yeah, whatever." I walked away, leaving Ian glaring at Nathanial in my stead.

"I'll never understand him," I muttered aloud.

"Understand who?"

I looked up at Scott. "Nathanial," I replied absently.

Although we had known each other for less than a week, I had put my trust in Scott. In my business, we had to trust each other; our lives were on the line. Nathanial and Ian treated him with respect, and Amy—who was probably my female best friend already—thought the world of him.

But, there was something about him, something...just a little off, that made me hesitate. Glancing at him from the corner of my eye, it finally hit me.

I couldn't sense his natural power that identified him as a Rytra.

He must have noticed me staring, for he gave me a friendly look and asked, "Something on my face?"

"Scott..." Hesitating, my eyes then widened with relief. "Never mind," I said. "For a minute, I couldn't sense your power. But it's okay now."

"Really? Well, at least all's well now." He laughed. "Still, you shouldn't need to sense someone's power, Jo, to trust them."

"Oh, no. Please, don't get the wrong idea," I hurriedly tried to amend the situation. "I'm paranoid; don't pay me any mind at all."

His smile didn't reach his eyes. "We all tend to be paranoid in this job, no?"

But walking through the hallways, I couldn't shake the feeling of uneasiness. How could Scott's Rytra Light just vanish and reappear like that? We who are tied to the elements could sense it in others. Suddenly Scott seemed a normal man walking by my side, not a Rytra. But the next moment he was Scott Peterson, Rytra, again.

We had reached Room 203 where our Sayta, Steven August slept. Finding his name printed on a dry cleaning receipt in his pocket had been a stroke of luck. Sayta didn't usually carry identification.

I turned to Scott. "Okay, why did you need me to come again? You never actually told me."

"Oh, didn't I?" said Scott innocently. "My dear Jo," he began while guiding me to a seat by the bedside, "you are here to delve into Mr. August's mind."

I stared at him open-mouthed. When I finally got my voice back, I exploded. "Are you crazy? Going into someone's mind is one of the most dangerous things in the world! Do you know how many people have been permanently damaged by attempting this? And not only the patient but the person doing the delving has been injured, too!"

Scott regarded me seriously. "Yes, I do know all that. But this could be the secret to finding out something about our enemies and their purpose. Don't you see, Jo? If you succeed, we might be able to defeat the Sayta. You are one of the best there is—if you can't do it, then no one can." He gave a small shrug. "But, if you don't want to, I'll understand."

My mind began weighing the pros and cons. There was the fact that this could help us immensely. And besides, didn't my job involve risks? Right. With a sigh, I placed my fingers lightly on August's forehead. "I've got to be absolutely blooming crazy to try this," I muttered.

"Aren't we all?" Scott asked. "You do know what to do, right?"

I wanted to roll my eyes but managed to hold myself in check. Still, when I spoke, my voice was almost snappish. "Yes, I know what to do."

To go into the mind of another person, you first had to break down their barriers. That in itself was hard. To top it off, when you entered the other mind, you were no longer aware of your own body. You didn't know when you were weakened and close to exhaustion. That's why during a mind delve a warrior could be seriously hurt or even die. It was wise to have another Rytra with you to help if necessary. If Scott hadn't been there, I wouldn't have attempted it.

After breaking down the walls, you could search the person's memories. Unless you actually stepped into the memory itself, you would only see flashes of images. It was a rich treasure trove, but like all treasure, a fierce fire-breathing dragon guarded it.

Taking a deep breath, I let my body fade away as I called upon the elements. I implored water to help me enter the place right before the barriers of his mind. As I lost feeling with the outside world, I became conscious only of task ahead. Before me was a high barrier made of earth, the Sayta equivalent of water. Behind that barrier, I could sense his thoughts and memories. Once the barriers were gone, it would be a piece of cake. Of course, I could die in the process, or the memories of the Sayta could be too horrible and dark for my Rytra soul to handle and I could go insane. Cheery consequences weren't they?

Imploring the water to do my bidding, I began to chip

away at the wall. It was a lot harder than I had thought and I did not know how much exertion I was using. I had to judge when I should stop, when I wouldn't be able to take any more. Timing and knowing your limit were crucial. But it was also mainly pure guesswork.

Just when I was thinking of giving up, a deep crack appeared. I used the water to smash into that weak spot repeatedly. After a moment, a large hole appeared and I carefully entered Steven August's mind.

It was dark. Shivering slightly, I slowly moved among his memories, searching for anything that could be of use. The memories appeared as silver-whitish bubbles one could step into. Memories glinted inside, rapidly flickering through scenes. It was possible to erase a memory by popping the bubble, but that was a dangerous job. Those who specialized in that were called Searchers, and they were few and far between. Some had a peculiar calling to the art that was "bubble-popping."

I didn't want to use up all of my energy here in this place, and I didn't want to hurt August. He was a Sayta, but he was our prisoner and if he was permanently damaged, then he would be of no more use to us. And, of course, my superiors would so not be happy.

And then I saw it. I froze in horror, staring in wide-eyed amazement. My common sense said I should get away quickly, but the practical part told me this memory was what I was looking for. I could see flickering images and hear a cold voice:

"We don't have the stone, and the Rytra are getting suspicious."

The voice was male and agitated, but otherwise unremarkable. The stone? The same stone that Joe Year was supposed to get? I was hearing a conversation regarding the current crisis. It was almost too good to be true.

"Be patient, my friend." A vaguely familiar male voice chuckled, "We will have everything soon enough. And won't it be grand?"

What will be grand? I had to hear more. Gathering my nerves, I walked into the memory. The bubble felt strange. I was expecting to be in some dark place, where I could hear the rest of the conversation. Unfortunately, after I took two steps into the memory… I found myself face to face with Steven August.

My mouth fell open and I stared. "What——?" Then I noticed how he seemed to be underwater; his form constantly wavered and wasn't very clear. "Oh. Just a mental image of yourself."

He grinned. "Very astute of you, Miss Whitwalker."

"But you're supposed to be comatose," I stated.

"While my body does sleep, my mind remains clear and perceptive," he replied.

"But if you're awake mentally, why did you let me enter your mind, August?"

Surprise flickered across his face. "How did you find out my name?" Although his voice was almost nonchalant, his eyes narrowed. An alarm bell in my head was blaring: *Warning! Warning! Back away from the angry man! I repeat, back away, now!*

"I let you enter because your defeat would be much more pleasurable if you suffered along the way."

I snorted. "You just couldn't repel me, you big liar."

For a moment, he looked very much like a wolf. "Maybe," He gestured around him. "But to more important matters. I set this memory up especially for you."

"Is it possible to fake a memory?" I asked.

His grin broadened. "Oh no, this is a real memory, my dear. I simply made sure you saw it."

I was confused. Why would he want me to see his memories?

"You see," August went on, "this is merely a memory of when I first found my powers and met my superior. Yes, it might allow you to see those who are above me, but I doubt very much that you'll be able to remember anything when you leave."

"Oh really? Well, let me tell you, buster, I have a pretty good memory," I snapped. Despite my words, I was not feeling confident. Not at all.

"Not after I'm through with it," he whispered.

I suddenly realized how close he was. Suddenly I found it impossible to move. "You see," he continued, "this is my mind. I control everything that goes on in here. I can easily go into your mind, find your most terrible memories, and make you relive them again and again. By the time I'm done, you won't have the mental capacity to tell the Rytra anything."

I had once read of a strange case in which the man whose memories were being invaded managed to repulse his attacker by bringing out the attacker's most painful memories. I didn't know how it worked, but apparently August did.

Not if I have any say in the matter. I tried to strike out,

reaching for the Light, but it was far away and I couldn't grasp it.

Before I could do anything else, there was a new presence in my mind—the presence of a memory.

The wailing of sirens filled the air. I stared around me in horror, eyes wide and stinging in the smoky air. "Davy?" I shouted. The scene of the crash was horrible. The cars involved were both totaled. All I wanted was to see my younger brother safe and sound. It really wasn't that much too ask for, was it? "Davy!" I shouted again.

A paramedic came up to me. "Excuse me, miss, but are you related to David Whitwalker?"

"Yes," I cried, relieved to find someone to help me. "I'm his older sister." I looked behind him, searching through the mass of people for the familiar sight of my 14-year-old brother. "Where is he?"

"Please come with me, Miss Whitwalker."

My heart jumped into my throat and stayed there. "What's wrong?" I asked as I hurried at his side. The paramedic did not respond.

He walked up to a stretcher. Upon it lay a man of 32 or so. It was Mr. Jones, our neighbor who carpooled with us. My face went deathly white; I could feel the blood draining from it. "No," I gasped. But I knew it to be true.

Mr. Jones was bringing four boys, including Davy, home from school today. They had been a block away from home.

The paramedic brought me to another stretcher, this one currently being loaded into the ambulance. I ran to it, grasping for my brother. "Davy!"

His brown eyes fluttered open for a minute. "Jo?" he whispered.

Grabbing his hand, I held it tightly. "Davy... oh no... please no..."

The paramedic tapped me on the shoulder. "Are your parents' home?" he asked.

I wiped away the tears with my sleeve, dirty from softball practice, but they just kept flowing. "Y-yes..." I gave him the phone number.

Another paramedic asked, "Are you coming to the hospital, miss?"

I nodded, my fingers tightening on Davy's hand. "Yes."

It was late. I sat alone in Davy's dark little hospital room, still clutching his hand. I wasn't sure if I was even allowed to be here this late, but the nurse that checked in every now and then said nothing. Since that moment right before he had been taken into the ambulance, Davy had remained unconscious. My parents and I had all waited anxiously for anything at all that would let us know Davy would make it. The doctor, however, was not at all positive. He said that Davy was suffering from internal bleeding and a broken back. Even if he did make it, he wouldn't be able to walk again. Still, Mum and Dad were hopeful. That hope suffered a terrible blow, however, when Mr. Jones died five hours after arriving at the hospital.

Everybody said that there was nothing to do but wait. The nurses said that we should go home and get some rest. I refused to go home; if anything happened, I would be here. I was, by far, closest to Davy. We talked about anything and everything. He had always been there for me, and now I would be there for him. Even if it all turned out for naught, I would be there.

"Oh, Davy," I whispered, gently stoking his limp hand. "Please don't die, Davy." Tears slipped down my cheek. I shut my eyes tightly, hunching over his still form. A broken sob shook me, tearing through my feeble defenses. "Please," I continued. "If there is anything good in the world, please, don't let Davy die." I willed someone, something, to help him with all my heart and soul.

I had never wanted something so strongly as I did in that single moment. I don't know when I noticed that my hands were wet. Blinking in confusion, I stared at them. I stumbled up from the hospital chair. Looking at Davy, I noticed that his hand I had been clutching was also wet. And then I realized how tired I was. At first, I thought it was the exhaustion of being up so late. But I could not shake the feeling that something had happened just now. Something very, very important.

The voice was barely audible. But I heard it. With a sob, I threw myself next to the bed, grasping the no-longer limp hand.

"Jo...why are you crying?" he whispered in confusion.

"Oh thank God... you're alive."

Davy made a full recovery, much to the astonishment of the doctors. Three days later, George Luen, my soon-to-be trainer, sought me out and told me that I was a Rytra: one who could control the Light. If the incident at the hospital hadn't happened, I never would have believed him. I began training to try to be one of the best Rytra ever. I worked so hard for fear that; otherwise, a day would come when I couldn't protect the people I loved. I had almost lost Davy once; I had no plans for that to happen again.

Although Davy had survived and I had discovered the calling on my life, that memory became one of my worst. The fear, the utter helplessness, and the knowledge that only my powers kept him alive often haunted me at night. It had been a miracle: a true and utter miracle. But, no matter how things had turned out, I hated that memory. I would often wish I could just forget it.

"No..." I gasped. "No more." Tears streamed down my face, but I didn't notice. I didn't notice anything but the pounding of my heart. I had vividly relived that crisis and all its emotions, especially the knowledge that Davy had almost been lost to me forever.

Steven August grinned. "Is this a painful memory, then?" His voice was cruel, and filled with amusement at my sufferings. "Well, shall we go round again?"

"No..." I cried, shivering.

But he paid my pathetic plea no mind. Once again memory overwhelmed me.

The wailing of sirens filled the air. I stared around me in horror...

TEN

Rude Awakening

I awoke so suddenly I was disoriented. "Davy!" I cried instinctively. Through wild eyes I saw that I was lying on a white bed with blue walls around me. A hospital room! That only increased my panic. All I could think of was Davy. Before I could jump out of bed in search of my little brother, strong but gentle hands gripped my shoulders, pushing me back into the pillows. I looked up into blue eyes.

"Nathanial?"

He smiled slightly. "Calm down, Jo," he said in a soothing voice.

Taking deep breaths, I felt my heart slow down to its normal rate again, and my thoughts began clearing. "What happened?" I murmured. The beeping from strange machines filled the air, making me edgy. There was an IV in my arm, the clear fluid dripping steadily from the bag near the bed. "The last thing I remember is Davy and the car accident. Where is he?"

Nathanial gave me a strange look. "I don't know what you're taking about, but I can tell you roughly what happened."

"Then stop babbling and do so."

His familiar smile disappeared quickly as he started

talking. "I decided to join you at the hospital about an hour after we parted ways. When I got here, I found you slumped over August, unconscious and close to dead." He gave me a stern look. "You should have known better than trying to go into his mind when you were by yourself."

I stared at him. "But Scott was here!" I protested.

Nathanial gave me another strange look. "Your mind must be playing tricks on you because Scott came right to RODD after dropping you off."

I started shaking my head, but the pain made me stop. "No!" I said angrily. "He was here with me when I went into August's mind. He was the one who wanted me to do it!" The truth began to dawn on me—the horrible truth that left me feeling numb. "Scott must have left right after I went into his mind!" I murmured.

Nathanial gave me a pitying look. "I think August messed with your mind more than you think he did, Jo. Scott would never do that," he said, his voice strangely gentle. It was like he was talking to a small child. "He said that you wanted to stay here by yourself, to see if August would wake up."

"So you're taking his word over mine?"

The look this time was both stern and pitying. "Yes, Jo. Right now, you're technically mentally unstable. I'm sorry, but we can't trust everything you say."

I was so stunned that I merely stared at him. I had begun to think of Nathanial as a good friend. His not trusting me was like a stab in the back. I rolled over onto my side so that my back was toward him. "Fine," I snapped. "You won't believe me. So why don't you do both of us a favor and just leave me alone."

"Jo…"

I didn't respond.

Blood was splattered across the floor and the walls. I stared around me in horror. Then I saw the body leaning against the wall, eyes wide and glassy with death. And I realized I had killed him.

Sliding to my knees, I buried my head in my hands, heedless of the blood on them.

"You're going to have to get used to it," said a hard, cold voice.

I looked up at my trainer, George Luen, who had agreed to accompany me back to America and finish my training there. His black eyes caught and held mine, merciless. "You're a Rytra now, Whitwalker. You are being trained to fight and kill Sayta." He motioned to the dead man. "And he was a Sayta. He deserved to die. He wouldn't have allowed you to take him captive. One of you had to die today. And if it had been you, that's one less Rytra to fight against the Dark. You didn't just fight for your own survival, Whitwalker. You fought for the survival of the world, for innocents."

"That doesn't make it any easier," I croaked.

George gave me a hard look. "Don't worry; you'll get used to it in time. So, buck up and get on with your life, Whitwalker."

Slowly, very slowly, I rose and followed George outside to clean up.

But I never once believed that I would get used to it.

My eyes shot open and I stared blankly at the ceiling. It was night now, the room bathed in soft moonlight. I was shaking badly. Memories could do that to people. I had been 18, alone and away from my family, the day I had killed that man. Eighteen was much too young for killing. And yet…I had. If I hadn't, others would have died. I had pushed those conflicting emotions to the back of my mind, locking them away with my most horrible memories. But now that August had laid bare the memory with Davy that had started the chain of events that changed my life forever, I had a feeling my memories were back to haunt me again.

I sat up, slowly and clasped my hands tightly together to try to quell the shaking. It didn't work. "Is this how it's going to be?" I murmured to myself. "Will my nights always be haunted by those dreams? I don't think I'd be able to handle that. And with no one believing me…" I realized I was crying. "Curse you, George Luen. And you, August. Curse everybody involved with the Sayta. You have made my life miserable."

A hand covered my own. My eyes shot open and I turned to stare at Nathanial. He took my hands in his, enclosing them in wonderful warmth. "It'll be all right," he murmured. His deep voice was soft, but I heard it perfectly. "You'll be fine. If I know you at all, Jo, you'll be able to face any challenges. Even your own demons."

Usually I hated it when I cried or people saw me crying. But tonight it didn't matter. The warm, salty tears would not stop flowing as an arm was wrapped around my shoulders, hugging me close to a warm, comforting body.

All my anger towards Nathanial dissipated, flowing away with the tears.

Eventually I drew away, wiping my eyes. "Sorry," I mumbled. Of course, now I was acutely embarrassed.

"Don't be," was all he said, but it was enough. For a while, we just sat in comfortable silence. Then he asked, "Did you find out anything of importance?"

"No," I sighed. "August was waiting for me and forced me to relive my worst memories." I looked at him. "Nathanial, do you remember what August said before he attacked?" He didn't reply, so I went on. "He said that you knew something about that stone. Do you?" No response. "Nathanial Vene, I demand an answer. And be truthful."

His eyes looked straight into my own. "No, Jo," he said calmly. "I don't."

I relaxed. I trusted both Nathanial and Ian with all my heart; they wouldn't lie to me. I knew they wouldn't hurt me.

Just as I was about to fall asleep, I realized something. Nathanial was still holding one of my hands, and he didn't seem to want to let go. As sleep stole over me, I decided that I liked that. I liked it very much.

"Oh, Josephine, I was so worried!"
I winced, trying to ease the strangle hold on my neck. "Mum, I'm fine. Really."

"But you almost died!" she wailed. Her bottom lip trembled wildly, as if it had a life of its own. "If Nathanial hadn't come, you would be dead by now!"

Patting her back, I resisted the urge to roll my eyes. She's just worried about you, I reminded myself. Looking over her shoulder, I saw Davy and Ian looking at me gravely. Nathanial was home, sleeping, after sitting up in my hospital room all night.

At last my mother drew away, sniffing slightly. "I'm going to go get some tea," she announced. "What kind do you want, Josephine?"

I preferred coffee to tea, but since my mother thought

that coffee was barbaric, I tried not to drink it around her. "If they have peppermint tea, that would be great," I said.

Once the door shut behind her, the room seemed to lose a little of its tension. My lovable mother had a gift for making people stressed with her nervous energy.

I rolled my eyes as she left and made a huge show of flopping back onto the pillows piled high behind me. Davy smiled slightly. I suddenly realized that he was not uncomfortable about being in the hospital. He was acting this way because our places had been switched. Before he had been the one close to death. This time, it was me.

"Davy," I said gently, "it all worked out last time. Everything will be fine."

It was a lie, and we both knew it, but sometimes a lie can be more comfortable than facing the truth.

"We just have to face our mental demons, Jo," Davy said. "We can beat them. You can beat them. I know that you can do it. You have to have faith, Jo."

Faith. I have faith in God. But in myself? That's another matter entirely.

There were too many things for me to do. Walk the line between Light and Dark and still fight the Dark… It seemed impossible. Especially when I had so few answers.

But I smiled at Davy all the same and said, "Whatever you say." And who knew? Maybe he was right. Maybe I could do it.

Faith… that's all I needed. Faith.

A little bit after noon, I was sitting alone in my room wishing that the doctor had not insisted that I stay in bed for a few more days. At least the IV was gone. Except for the whole mental instability bit and the exhaustion, I was perfectly healthy.

"Good morning, Jo."

And with that single sentence, every muscle was alive, every nerve on edge.

Scott looked at me with amusement on his boyish features, smiling as if nothing in the world was wrong. As if he hadn't betrayed me, leaving me to die.

"What are you doing here?" I asked, more than a little coldly. Fear flooded my veins, swamping me until my chest tightened. But the Light was there, just out of reach and within grasp. I wasn't unprepared this time.

He smiled thinly. "I've merely come to see how you are recovering."

"If you hadn't left, I wouldn't need to recover," I snarled.

His eyes narrowed. When he spoke, however, his voice was calm and soothing, as if he was talking to a child. "What are you talking about, my dear Jo?"

"You came with me to the hospital, made me go into August's mind, and then left me to die," was my furious reply.

"I didn't come with you to the hospital. You wanted to be alone with August."

"Liar!"

"What if I am?" he asked oddly. At that moment, I came to the conclusion that I was right about Scott…he wasn't on the side of Light. The way he was looking at me, the glimmer in his eyes…he had tried to kill me, no matter what others said. "What are you going to do about it?" He gave a chuckle, a satisfied smirk playing across his lips. "Did you know they are thinking of putting you in an asylum for a while?"

I gritted my teeth. "At whose urging, I wonder?"

Again he laughed. "No one trusts you, Jo. You went through a great ordeal; everyone understands you aren't in your right mind now."

Without another word, he walked out of the room. I was left alone with my thoughts which are, perhaps, a person's worst companions.

ELEVEN

To Reach August

"All right," I murmured softly to myself, "Think, Jo. What do you know? Well, I know that no one trusts me and probably won't listen to a word I say. Congratulations, the award goes to Jo Whitwalker for Understatement of the Year Award. Judging from the way Scott is acting, he is obviously working against the Rytra so, he must not really be one. But that still leaves me with the question of how he uses Rytra powers. I saw him at the transportation. I didn't imagine his powers then.

"Why me? Why do I have to deal with all this stuff? Why do I have to walk the line between Dark and Light and restore the balance?" The ceiling did not answer. "Well, you certainly have been helpful, Mr. Ceiling. Thanks."

"You seem to be feeling better," Nathanial said sarcastically as he stepped into the room.

"Yeah," Ian scrutinized me. "Or is this feistiness from some sort of medication they've been giving you?"

I rolled my eyes. "Yes, Ian, that must be it," I drawled. "Why else would I act like this?" I sat up, looking at them intently. "So, have you guys just come to abuse me, or do you have some kind of information?" I directed my comments at Nathanial.

"Our original plan was just a friendly visit, but some interesting developments have come up," he replied.

My curiosity was piqued. "What?"

"August is awake."

My eyebrows rose. "Not one for beating around the bush, are you?" I threw off my sheets, swinging my legs over the side of the bed.

"What are you doing?" both men asked in unison.

I gave them a "no-duh" look. "Getting out of bed and dressing," I said in a slow voice, as if talking to a child.

"But you're still weak," Nathanial argued.

I wanted to tell him I wasn't, but I couldn't. As soon as I stood up, my head rocked. I had been in bed for days, and still I wasn't completely healed. But I wanted to see August. Childish? Yes. Did I care? No.

"I'll make it," I replied grimly.

Ian pulled a long-sleeved t-shirt and pants from my suitcase. Smiling, I took them and shooed them out so I could change. Changing left me surprisingly weak and pale, and made my two partners exchange worried glances. But, noting the determination on my face, they said nothing.

I have pride. Everyone does. So as we walked down the hospital hallway at a hobble, I did not ask for help. I was weak and slow, but I used the wall for support, not my friends. Foolish of me, perhaps, but hey, a girl has to have some dignity. Of course, some would argue that it was a lot less dignified to lean against a wall than a person, but those people don't know what they're talking about.

When we finally did reach August's room, a nurse was just coming out of it. Unfortunately, I knew the nurse. She was one of those who were positive that I was off my rocker. Her eyes narrowed at me, but I glared back. "Is Mr. August awake?" I asked.

"Yes," she said coldly.

I started towards the door, keeping one wary eye on the intimidating lady and one on where I was going.

"But you can't see him," she said with a smug cat-like look on her face. "Mr. August is still very weak. He is not to be disturbed today or tomorrow. Too much excitement is dangerous for him."

Now, I could have come up with a lot of comebacks. But did I? No. Because, unlike others, I actually am a nice person. Relatively speaking, of course. And I had a feeling that this nurse could put me to sleep in my present condition. And I was not sure if it was the sleep-sleep kind or the death-sleep kind.

"You aren't supposed to be out of bed either, Miss Whitwalker," the nurse continued sternly. She advanced a step. Despite myself, I took a step back, which made my head rock very alarmingly.

I turned my back on her to walk to my room. It was at this time that my legs buckled beneath me, much to my alarm. Hey, you aren't supposed to do that! I scolded them silently. My head was whirling almost too much to think, and I felt faint. One hand was on the wall in an effort to slow my descent. When my head cleared a few seconds later, I found strong, sure arms around me. My body was pressed against another's, and it was nice and warm. Slowly looking up, the blood began to drum in my ears as my eyes met Nathanial's.

As if I was nothing but a kitten, he was carrying me in his arms. "Hey, I'm all right!" I protested weakly. "I can walk."

Nathanial snorted. "Yeah, right. Stop acting like a child, Jo."

I blushed and shut my mouth.

"Maybe next time you'll listen to us, eh, Jo?" Ian said from the side.

I looked at him. Although his tone was light, there was something in his eyes that brought me up short. I actually recognized and understood this emotion. It was jealousy. Ian was jealous? Over what?

Nathanial and me, the little voice in the back of my head whispered to me. *He wants to be the one holding you, not Nathanial.*

But that's crazy! I argued with myself. *We're just friends!*

After the two had left, I analyzed the situation logically. I knew that Ian was good at hiding his feelings. Once he went a week being depressed and none of us ever guessed. The only reason I found out was because he told me. And Ian did act friendly towards me. I always pictured us as friends; hence the use of the term "friendly." The conversation with Nathanial on the plane popped into my mind. He had wondered if Ian and I were closer than just friends. What if he noticed something that I didn't? Ian was a friend: that's all he would ever be, at least in my book. But the possibility that he liked me that way wasn't out of the question. *Was it?*

I was so confused. There were too many feelings whirling around inside me. I have liked very few guys in my lifetime, and even fewer have liked me. None of them were my best friend. What was I supposed to do in a situation like this? I didn't know, and the sheer frustration of everything was nearly enough to bring tears to my eyes.

Of course, I could be reading way too much into this. But there was really no way to tell unless Ian said something. So, I guessed, only time would tell.

With a groan, I pulled a pillow over my head. *Why couldn't life ever be easy?*

TWELVE

Somebody by my Side

It was the day after attempting to visit August, and I was trying to get some sleep. Instead of peaceful rest and relaxation, I was having disturbing dreams. More memories. At least I woke quickly.

Ian didn't appear to notice that I had awakened, so I was able to observe him. His eyes were flickering over me, as if trying to capture every detail. His eyes were surprisingly gentle and caring, far more than I had ever seen before. It made me uneasy.

"Ian?" I murmured.

"You're such a heavy sleeper," he immediately joked, leaning back in his chair. "I'm surprised your own snores didn't wake you."

I glared at him, easily putting on the face that said I was normal. It really was a face this time, though. For, despite the fact that everything seemed the same with me and Ian, my heart told me differently.

It told me that he loved me… and I wouldn't be able to return the feeling.

Ian had gone back to RODD several hours ago, and I was trying to stay interested in a mystery novel. I'd read the same page several times. The door opened and I looked up.

"Hey, Nathanial," I called, putting my book on the nightstand.

He smiled slightly. "Hey."

I realized suddenly that there were dark circles under his eyes, as if he had been getting little or no sleep. "You look tired," I said sternly.

Whatever he was expecting, it wasn't that. He blinked, and I could have sworn that he started to blush. "I've been up late working," he replied. He sat down on the edge of my bed. "Jo," he murmured, "I've been thinking a lot about what you said. About Scott. And how I wouldn't trust you."

My breath hitched in my throat. What was he getting at...?

"I think I believe you," he whispered. His eyes were on mine. "I really do."

"Why?" I heard myself ask. My world was spinning, but this time it was for happiness, in anticipation that, maybe, I wouldn't be alone in this after all.

His eyes were frank. "Because I trust you."

He didn't need to say anything else. He believed me and he was with me completely. That's all that mattered. "Thank you," I told him, just as quietly.

He nodded, and we sat in silence for a moment, dwelling in a happy peace that I knew would all too soon be destroyed. Indeed, Nathanial broke the stillness by standing, taking out his cell phone. "We need to talk," he said. "I'll call Ian to get down here."

I looked up. "And Amy," I added. He glanced at me, one eyebrow raised slightly. I smiled. "We can trust her," I said without hesitation. Amy would never betray us. She was too good, too pure, for that.

Apparently Amy and Ian were together at the office. Nathanial only had to make one call. He was very short and abrupt. He did, however, direct them not to tell Scott anything. When one of them asked why, he simply said, "Just don't" and hung up.

While Nathanial waited outside the door, I got dressed. I felt stronger, partly because it felt wonderful to have someone at my side.

Ian and Amy arrived shortly, both looking worried. Ian placed a hand on my arm. "Are you okay?" he asked.

There was more in his eyes than a friend's simple worry. And, for a moment, everything faded away as my world narrowed down to Ian and his feelings for me. What would I do if he did tell me? What would I say to him?

I had no idea. I didn't want to hurt him; no matter what, he was my best friend. But I couldn't lie, either. *Why don't you like him?* my traitorous, logical brain asked. *He's nice, good looking, and you know without a doubt that you can trust him.*

But I don't love him, I replied silently.

Why not?

Why not? Why didn't I love him? Best friends often fell in love. Why not us?

Without really realizing it, my eyes flickered over to Nathanial, who was explaining the situation to Amy and Ian. I felt my cheeks flush. *Snap out of it, Jo!* I silently yelled at myself. *Why would you look at him anyway?*

"Jo?"

"Wha—?" was my brilliant reply.

"Now that Jo has joined us again," quipped Nathanial dryly, "maybe she can tell us what we do now." Ian and Amy looked at me with complete trust.

"Ian, Nathanial, and I will go see August," I slowly said. "All of this is tied together—the Sayta, the stone, and Scott. August knows something; I'm sure of it. Amy, can you stay here and stave off any questions from the nurses?"

She nodded.

The walk to August's room was silent as we all dwelt on our private thoughts and fears, on our anger at Scott's betrayal, and wondering about what would happen next. At least, that's what I thought about it.

Our thoughts were rather painfully shattered when we came to August's room... and found that we weren't alone.

"What are you people doing?"

I winced. Yes, you guessed it. It was my friend, the nurse.

"Look, Miss Nurse, I'm through playing your games. We have a job to do, and we intend to do it, whether you want us to or not! So don't interfere."

Without a word, she turned and marched off.

We watched her retreating back, before turning to each other again. "Ready?" I asked. Before they could reply, I took a deep breath and opened the door.

August was lying on the bed on his back, his head turned toward the window. "Hey, you awake?" I asked, rather rudely, nudging the bed with my foot.

No response.

I moved over so I could see his face. August's eyes were opened, but unseeing. His throat had been slit. The blood that covered the sheets was so vivid that it almost looked fake. The knife that had done the deed was on the bedside table. No doubt the handle was wiped clean of fingerprints. Closing his eyes, I said, "He's dead."

"Of course," Nathanial murmured. "Scott wouldn't want him to talk."

I sighed. Our luck could not get any worse.

I stood still trying to think of what to do. My head was whirling and when the door flew open, it certainly did nothing for my taut nerves.

The nurse stood there, glowering darkly. She immediately spotted the blood and let out a piercing shriek. Two other nurses, a doctor, and security came running. They stared; we stared back. They were civilians, after all, and we were never to get innocents involved. It was like the old code of chivalry: war was solely between soldiers and never the civilians. We Rytra and Sayta were the soldiers, and these people were the civilians. We couldn't try to escape without causing them harm, and escaping itself would be near impossible without use of the elements.

The security men went into action. The next thing I knew, my arms were pinned to my body. They didn't give us a chance to explain. The security men marched us all down the hallways of the hospital. People stared at us, and whispers spread through the building. How could they accuse us of murder without letting us speak? Of course, most of us in the group had killed before, me included. Maybe all that blood on our hands was finally catching up to us.

The elevator dinged to a halt and opened. We were led out of the space and into a deserted hallway. Unlike the ones below it, it was carpeted and short. There were only a few doors, and most of those had a nameplate on the outside. Offices, then. We were led into one without anything on the door. Inside were three couches and a table. Despite the faded blue carpet and the dark green walls, the room was not warm. They sat us down on the couches and told us to keep quiet.

Everything was so confusing, so hard. It was all Scott and the Sayta's fault. And yet we were being blamed for it. That stupid stone they kept talking about was in the forefront of this mess. I had almost forgotten about that stone. What was so important about it? I shot a sidelong glance at Nathanial. And why did August accuse Nathanial of knowing something about it? Did he? Was he lying to me? My anger rose, almost to the point of being unbearable.

If only I could leave, forget about all this and go back to a semi-regular life. But I couldn't ever do that. Not with everything that was going on. I was ensnared in this, whether I liked it or not. Well, first things first. Getting out of this little ugly spot with the police. And that would probably take a while. After that, we had to find the stone or information on the stone. We had to.

Three police officers came in, as well as Scott.

Every muscle went tense. Scott? What in the world was he doing here? If anything, he would probably find it a lot easier if the police convicted us of murder. Nathanial's eyes narrowed in distaste, and he never looked away from Scott.

Ian just sat on the couch, slumped with his eyes half closed. Thinking, maybe. But no… Ian would look at Scott as well. He wouldn't continue to think with his eyes closed. It was only then that I realized Ian was humming with power. He had summoned some of the elements! My mouth must have fallen open, for I felt myself slowly closing it. What was he going to do? He couldn't attack civilians. Surely he wouldn't.

"Are these your co-workers, Mr. Peterson?" asked one of the policemen.

For a minute his eyes flashed dangerously. "Yes," Scott said.

What was he doing? Why was he helping us? It all became clear a minute later.

"Yes, these people are the ones I told you about. The ones who murder. I believe they're part of a cult who believe in human sacrifices. And now you have proof." He spoke to the nurse who had first seen us in August's room. "You were with Steven August before his death, correct?"

The nurse nodded. "Yes, sir. And he was alive." Her words were like curses.

"And you saw them enter his room. No one else entered or left, correct?"

"Correct."

"So, it is obvious that they are the only ones capable of this." Triumph shone in his eyes. "I have had my doubts about them; now I'm certain of it. They are murderers."

And it wasn't a lie. We had killed before. If put to a lie detector, Scott would technically be telling the truth. We had underestimated him, and now we were paying the price. At that moment, I've never wanted to kill anyone more. If only I could wrap my fingers around his throat and squeeze until I lost all feeling in my hands.

But I couldn't help but think what Scott would do now. Everyone at RODD knew about August and the fact that he was a Sayta. They obviously couldn't come to our rescue, but what would they do when they learned that Scott had handed us over? Would they refuse to follow him anymore? They might even kill him. It was a possibility. And what exactly was Scott? As I stared at him now, I was positive that he was not a Rytra.

Smirking at us, Scott left, followed by the nurse and one policeman.

"You guys are coming with us," growled another of the policemen.

Ian's eyes snapped open. "I have had enough of this," he said, his voice deadly calm and cold enough to make an iceberg appear warm. It even scared me. He suddenly released the power of the elements. I raised an arm to cover my eyes, wincing at the bright light. When it faded, all of the guards were unconscious on the ground.

"Let's go get Amy and get out of here," said Nathanial.

We started out the door and ran into her. "Oh, you're all right!" she gasped. "I was so worried."

"Well, we're okay for now," I said. "Let's get out of here. My family needs to be warned, and we need to find a safe place. I'm sure Mum will know one."

Ian and Nathaniel looked at me with complete trust. Amy never wavered once. I wondered how the upcoming trials would change them—if they would survive.

Or even if I would survive.

THIRTEEN

Safe Haven

Naturally, getting out wasn't easy.

The four of us piled into the large elevator. "Right," said Ian, rubbing his hands together grimly. "Do we use the elements to shield us?"

Nathanial was frowning. "It'll take a lot of power to shield us all," he mused.

Amy frowned. "And my car isn't exactly nearby. Even if we are invisible, we will have to take care not to bump into anyone. It'll take a while and a lot of power."

"Then we use power," I snapped. "Ian, Nathanial, and I will do the shielding."

"No," Amy stated flatly. "You look pale, Jo dear. You still haven't fully recovered, have you?"

I scowled at her.

"I thought so. No, you will be making sure we don't bump into anyone. I'm sure the boys and I will be able to put up a fine shield."

I started to argue. "Stop fighting those who wish to protect you," Nathanial said.

The elevator dinged, the doors sliding open. Immediately Amy, Nathanial, and Ian called upon the air. With a whirl it surrounded us, shielding us from human eyes. Amy led the way, her back straight, and her stride confident. I quickly followed until I had fallen in step with her. Nathanial and Ian came behind us, concentrating wholly on their job. It was one thing to make a simple barrier, and quite another to make the barrier extend its invisibility over us. Ian was sweating profusely, and I realized suddenly that he must be exhausted. After all, he was the one who had knocked the guards out. He must be reaching into his last reserves of strength.

That walk seemed to be forever, but we made it to Amy's car, a 2003 Chrysler, without any problems. Dismissing the element, Amy climbed in the driver's seat. Nathanial got into the passenger side, and Ian and I took the back.

We drove in silence. We didn't want to talk about Scott, or the Sayta, or the threat to the Rytra that hung over our heads. My whole world was coming down around my ears. We all knew that nothing would ever be the same again.

At long last we reached my house. There were no Sayta around, no feeling of the Dark. Breathing a sigh of relief, I let myself in.

"Mum?" I called out.

My mother came out. "Jo!" She looked at me, her eyes narrowing slightly. "Is this it, Josephine?" she asked quietly. "Is this the reason you came to England?"

"Yes, Mum."

She nodded, both thoughtful and sad. "All right. Let's get cracking, shall we?"

My mother is one of the most efficient packers I know. Within a few minutes she had stuffed two large overnight bags with food and given me money from the safe. We would no doubt need it before all this was over. Amy quickly explained what had happened, which made my mother's mouth become a thin, grim line.

"I know of an old, rundown hotel that you can stay in," Mum said, her voice crisp. "No one will think to look for you there. It should do for a safe haven."

"But what about you?" I cried. "You cannot stay here, not with Scott knowing about you! He won't hesitate to use you against me."

"Don't worry," she said, patting my hand. "As soon as you are out of here, I'm packing up the family. We'll stay with your Aunt Penny in Scotland until this is all over. She's almost a recluse, so I doubt anyone will be able to find us. There is a RODD near there if we need help."

"Mum," I started, and then fell silent. I wanted to tell her what she meant to me, just in case ....

Her eyes softened. "It's all right, Josephine," she said, gathering me in a fierce embrace. "I know."

"Thank you," I whispered. It was horribly inadequate, but the best I could do. "Say goodbye to everyone for me, okay?"

"Of course, dear." She kissed my forehead.

With supplies in the trunk, we piled in the car. Mum gave Amy instructions on how to reach Hotel Fairdown, on the far side of a small forest by a lake. Scenic.

"They'll be all right," Nathanial said softly. Blinking back tears, I hoped with all my heart he was right.

We took a roundabout route to Hotel Fairdown. The road through the forest was nothing but dirt, filled with bumps that sent us careening against each other. It was overcast, thick gray clouds gathering like soldiers on a battlefield in the sky. It was rather eerie. A few birds sang out, but that was the only sign of life. Perhaps the animals could sense the impending storm as well.

We came out of the forest and all leaned forward, eager to see Hotel Fairdown. It was a crumbling stone building, large and imposing with ivy growing up the sides. Behind a cracked black sign that proclaimed the name of the hotel, the lake glistened blue-gray, rippling in the wind.

The inside was worse: dusty and covered in spider webs. I tried to banish the feeling that the whole structure would collapse on us. The less-than-cheerful atmosphere became more depressing as it began to rain. My mother had provided lots of flashlights and candles which became our only light. Amy and Ian began to clear away dust in one of the main rooms where we would spend the night, staying together for warmth, reassurance, and safety. Nathanial and I went exploring but found nothing of interest. The whole place, thankfully, was free of any feeling of the Sayta and the Dark.

Ian caught my eyes the moment Nathanial and I walked back into the room. He looked angry—which was rather disconcerting. Before I could say anything to him, he came up beside me. "Jo, a word?" He darted a glance at Nathanial, daring him to say anything. Nathanial didn't seem to notice the look or chose to ignore it.

"Um, sure." My voice was a little shaky. All I wanted to do was curl up on some bit of floor and go to sleep, but even that simple pleasure was being denied to me.

Ian led the way back up the steps, making me regret that this hotel had more than one story, and into the room farthest from the stairs. Rain drummed against the roof, deadening everything but the sound of the drops. I looked at the ceiling dubiously. "It had better not give in," I murmured. I was stalling and we both knew it. "What do you want to talk about, Ian?" I thought it best to act like I had no clue.

Ian shifted, uncomfortably. "Jo, we've been friends for a long, long time."

"Yeah…"

"And, well, I-I thi-think…" He paused. It kind of surprised me that he was stuttering. Ian never stuttered. He was hot-tempered, boyish, slightly sarcastic, but uneasy? Never.

"I think… I think…"

With my heart beating rapidly against my ribs, it was hard to concentrate. I was even becoming a little light-headed. *No*, part of me whispered. I had wanted to get this over with, but now I only wanted it to stop. *Please, Ian. Don't say anything. Because if you do, everything will change. And I don't want that to happen.*

"Jo, I think I've fallen in love with you!" he finally blurted out. His eyes, fiery and passionate, refused to look away.

The single, logical fiber in my being (and there probably was only one) was telling me that I shouldn't be so confused. That I should just tell him that I didn't feel the same way and get it over with, and pray that we could still be friends. But I couldn't bring myself to do it. I didn't want to hurt Ian. A hot, burning sensation was in my throat, and I swallowed several times trying to get rid of it. I couldn't lie to him, but I didn't want to tell him the truth either.

Once again, I thought of why I couldn't love Ian. Was it

possible that someone else had captured my heart? No, there couldn't be anyone else. Suddenly, I recalled the feeling of being so close to Nathanial at the hospital. He had been so warm, so comfortable; I had wanted to stay there forever. I had wanted to feel his arms around me.

Nathanial? I thought, my head spinning. *I love Nathanial?* It seemed so impossible, yet so probable at the same time. And I couldn't deny the feelings sweeping over me. I couldn't deny the thought that this feeling, this love, was completely and utterly *right*. That it couldn't be false.

"Jo?"

Ian was looking at me, his face both worried and hopeful. He must have noticed some emotion on my face. Uncertainty, then comprehension flashed in rapid succession.

It broke my heart all over again. I could almost feel the little pieces breaking away. "Oh, Ian…I'm so sorry," I sobbed. I wiped away the tears, shaking slightly. "I don't want to hurt you, Ian. Really. I love you… as a friend." I looked up into his eyes, reaching out instinctively to grab his hands. "Please, don't be mad at me." *Please don't hate me for not loving you. I want to, I really do.* And the funny thing was I did want to love him. I knew it would be a wonderful thing if I could. But no matter how much I told myself this, my feelings refused to change.

Ian sighed, rubbing his face with hands that shook. "I'm not mad at you, Jo," he finally admitted. "A little disappointed, but, hey, that's to be expected, right?" Another tear trailed down my cheek, and I wished I would stop crying. Ian's face softened, and he wiped away the tears. "Stop that," he chided gently. "There's no reason to be crying."

"But, but I—"

He put a finger to my lips, gently silencing me. "It's okay," he whispered, and truth was in every word.

I wrapped my arms around his waist, burying my head in his shoulder. I didn't really think of how it would make him feel. It was almost hard to believe that he wasn't angry with me. I would be heartbroken, furious with myself as well as bitterly disappointed in the other person. But no. Ian was just being Ian: gentle, caring, aware of others feelings, and not willing to force them into anything.

At last I pulled away, sniffing. "I'm sorry," I muttered again, wiping my nose.

Ian handed me his handkerchief. "Stop saying that," he commanded, but gently. "I'll be all right. I promise." For a minute, he was silent. "Is it... Nathanial?" he asked after a moment. He said the name as if it was something he didn't particularly care for.

I shifted. It was now my turn to be distinctly uncomfortable. "I-I'm not completely sure," I muttered. "But... I think so." I looked up, my eyes pleading. "Don't say anything to him, Ian. Please. And be nice, okay?"

Ian growled softly. "No, I won't be sayin' a thing. And since you're the one asking me, I'll be nice." He shook his head. "I can't say that I don't envy him, though."

I managed a weak grin. "Thank you, my little leprechaun."

I was trying to act like I used to with him, but we both knew that things would never be quite the same. We would get along fine and joke and tease just like we used to. But, in the back of our minds, there would be that constant reminder that he had once loved me and that I couldn't say that the feeling was mutual.

Amy was asleep when we came back. Nathanial looked up, his sharp eyes falling upon the tear tracks on my cheeks. Ian smiled and said, "Get some sleep."

Nathanial reached my side. "Are you okay?" he asked.

I smiled at the concern in his voice. "Yeah," I said, my heart fluttering again. Stupid thing. Why couldn't it just obey what I wanted? Why did it have to act on its own and give me all these feelings I didn't want?

"Night, Jo," Nathanial said, instead of questioning me further.

I sat down on the floor, drawing up one of the blankets my mother had given us around my shoulders. "Goodnight, Nathanial."

I turned my back on everyone, blocking them out, so I felt more alone with my thoughts. Closing my eyes, I concentrated on slowing my breathing. When I had accomplished that, I dove into the turmoil that was my feelings. If I didn't, I would be distracted, and that was simply not allowable.

I did not love Ian. That was obvious, established a long time ago. And now, at last, I was at peace with it. Ian wasn't angry at me, and I could finally relax a little. He was still my best friend and would always be there. But then there was the tiny little problem that I was almost positive that I was in love with Nathanial.

Even just thinking about it sent my heart into overdrive again. It was strange, seeing Nathanial in my mind as more than just a friend. Then I began to think of him: the way he watched out for all of us, the warmness of his body against mine, and his beautiful features. I giggled a little to myself, rather like a schoolgirl with her first kiss.

I'm in love, I thought, a little giddily.

With a tired, if rather pleased sigh, and that pleasant thought floating around in my head, I closed my eyes and concentrated instead on the steady, comforting drumming of rain on the roof. I fell asleep for what seemed like only a few minutes.

And woke to find myself in a living nightmare.

fine. After all, I'm the person who restored the balance between Rytra and Sayta, at least for the moment, so I seem to have some agility."

"Humph," he snorted slightly as I stumbled over a rock in the path. But his eyes gleamed with amusement and love.

"And besides," I said, gripping his hand tighter, "should I lose my balance and fall, I have you to catch me."

FOURTEEN

Nathanial's Story

Nathanial loomed above me, one hand on my shoulder as he shook me awake. His face was pale, his eyes glittering like dark gems. Fear! I never thought I'd see that emotion on his face! My own spirit trembled, wanting to back down. But I couldn't.

"What's happening?" I demanded, struggling to my feet.

A minute later the stench of Dark came over me.

"They're almost here," Nathanial whispered, seeing the look on my face.

I nodded and took a breath. I had been trained to handle myself—and others—in situations like this. There was no time to waste. "Ian, Amy!" I snapped.

Both immediately came to my side. Keeping my voice barely audible I said, "We can't stay here. The Sayta are after the stone. I doubt they'll let rest until we're dead."

"But we don't have the stone," growled Ian.

"Unfortunately, I have to contradict you," Nathanial said. "I have the stone."

We all stared at him in horror.

"So you're the reason they've come after us," Amy murmured.

There was a bit of shame on his face. "I'm sorry. But I just couldn't tell you."

Amy nodded, eyes wise and understanding. "I know."

"Look," I broke in impatiently, expecting a Sayta to burst in at any moment, "we can't stay here. We can't let them have that stone."

"Right," Nathanial said, already striding toward the door. "I hope to see you all in the future."

I stared at his back for a split second. "Whoa, whoa, stop right there!"

I wasn't protesting his leaving. We all knew that he had to so that the stone would not fall into Sayta hands. It wasn't running away; it was a tactical retreat. It was the whole going alone part that I didn't like.

"What, Jo?" His voice was harsh, cold. He was trying to hurt me, so I wouldn't do anything I would regret. Too late.

"You're not going alone."

At this he did turn. His eyes met mine, wide with surprise, then narrow with disagreement.

"We don't have any time for this!" I snapped before he could speak. "You can't go alone, Nathanial. I won't let you. I'm coming with you, whether you like it or not."

Ian watched us, his eyes darting back and forth. Then, apparently coming to a decision, he stepped forward. "I'll slow them down," he said.

I turned my attention to him, a protest on my lips. *You can't!* my mind screamed at him. *You'll die!* But the words would not go past the lump in my throat. Looking into his bright gray eyes, I nearly started crying. He was doing this—for me. For all of us. I wanted to say thank you. But that wasn't adequate. Not nearly.

"You'd better be alive when I come back for you," I said, my voice shaking.

He winked at me. "Of course, Jo. I wouldn't dream of not being alive."

"Amy, go to Scotland. Find my parents, and make sure they're okay. Then get reinforcements. There's a man in Seattle name Gerald Dyose—you can trust him and anyone who works under him."

Amy nodded and left quickly.

Taking a breath and forcing back tears, I darted forward, grabbing Nathanial's hand, and leading the way out of the back door of the hotel.

"Jo," Nathanial whispered to me, "you shouldn't be doing this."

"I've been doing things I shouldn't all my life."

It was dark, about midnight. The rain pounded against our bodies and into the soggy ground, a rapid beat that wouldn't stop. I was glad for it. The rain against my face hid tears that flowed down my cheeks. We ran for the lake.

"You can swim, right?" Nathanial yelled over the howl of the storm.

I nodded. Together we dove into the freezing lake. It would be hard to see us here, and the rain on the water concealed our splashing. We did not dare use the elements; the Sayta would sense the power and find us by tracking its source.

We were almost at the far bank when an incredible amount of magical energy surrounded the Hotel Fairdown behind us. Nathanial and I froze, eyes locked on the building. I couldn't stop the gasp of horror that ripped out of my throat.

The hotel was burning.

Flames licked towards the sky, like some twisted, macabre fireworks, eating eagerly away at the old, rotting boards and crumbling stone. Not even the rain could slow the burning. The pure, unrestrained element of fire was fueling it. Black clouds of smoke rolled off, rising steadily before the full moon. Even from this distance, I could hear shouts—men crying out to one another. Was one of those men Ian?

Without thinking, I called to the elements. I had to find out if he was alive. The next moment, it was like I was at the hotel. I could hear the crackling of the flames of the inferno. Then... voices. They pounded in my head. I would never forget them. Never.

"Well, if it isn't Ian McKinley," came Scott's cold voice.

"Surprise, Scotty boy. Aren't you happy to see me?" Ian shot back coldly.

"Yes, as a matter of fact, I am. Because now... I can kill you with my own hands." There was a short pause. "And my dearest Jo will watch the whole thing."

What? I yelled silently.

Then I could see both of them, standing in the midst of the red-orange flames. A barrier kept the fire from touching them. But I hardly noticed. All of my attention was on Ian as he stared defiantly at Scott. His eyes burned as fiercely as the fire around him. His chin was raised stubbornly. There was no fear on his face as he lashed out with all his physical and elemental might.

My vision turned fuzzy; I could only make out vague images. I waited tensely. Then... someone screamed. An image flashed through my mind: gray eyes wide with shock, filled with pain. A body slowly falling to the ground. Blood pooling around a motionless form on the ground. The fire licked at the edges of the dark red substance. And, above it all, was the sound of mocking laughter.

"NOOOOO!"

Forcefully jerked out of my inert state, I stared wildly at Nathanial. I was yelling something incoherent, unable to hear anything except that laughter ringing in my ears. Nathanial was saying something. I fought wildly, trying to free myself from his tight hold. Tears were streaming down my face.

"NO!" I was shouting. "Let me go! He's not dead! He can't be dead! No! He just can't be! Iaaaaaan!"

A sharp slap silenced me. I stared at Nathanial in shock, unable to believe he had just hit me. "Jo, stop it," he told me harshly. "I don't know what you saw, but if it was a Sayta, then you are doing just what they want! They want you to stay here for them to find us. And we cannot do that."

"But, Ian—!" No. He can't be dead. I have to get to him. I have to be with him.

"Later! We need to move, and now!"

Grabbing my hand, Nathanial dragged me along. Feeling as if my whole world was dissolving around me, I followed, stumbling and tripping. We ran into the woods. The tall trees shielded us from view, towering above us like monsters out of a fairy tale. The branches ripped at clothes and skin, tripping us, but somehow we managed to run on.

We didn't dare go into the city, not yet. Scott probably had people everywhere looking for us. We needed a place to hide, if only to catch our breath and think of a plan. I managed to fall into such a place. Literally. One minute the ground was beneath my feet, and the next, it simply wasn't. I found myself in a small, abandoned hidey-hole or animal snare. Rough soil walls formed it, and the ground beneath was littered with small bones. Still, it was the best there was at the moment.

"Jo?" Nathanial called hesitantly from above.

I stood, peering up at him. The walls were taller than I, but Nathanial probably wouldn't have any trouble hoisting himself up.

"Come on down," I said.

Apparently he, too, understood the need to stay hidden while coming up with a plan. He pulled some fallen branches partially on top of the hole to conceal it and slid through an opening. With both of us in the hole, it was cramped to say the least. We had to sit close together, our knees drawn partially up. I found myself tucked into the crook of Nathanial's arm. It made my face heat up, but I can't deny that I liked it. We were both soaking wet and shivering, but our combined body heat helped to warm us.

"You all right?" he asked.

Although I wasn't, I nodded. I wasn't anything even close to "all right."

"You?"

"Fine," was the very short reply.

I nodded into his shoulder, biting my lip slightly. I wanted to talk about the vision of Ian, but the stone was our top priority at this moment. "Nathanial, you have to tell me. Why do you have the stone?"

He didn't even protest. "I'll tell you the story of the stone and maybe you'll understand why I couldn't let anyone else know where it was," he began. "It's been in my family for generations. My ancestor, Gwyneth, created the stone in the Medieval Age. She was a Rytra who wanted to strengthen the influence of the Light because the Sayta were starting to outnumber the Rytra. She came up with the idea of using a stone as a vessel for filling the Sayta with Light— changing them to Rytra—hopefully.

"A group of her Rytra companions combined their powers with hers to help create the stone. Things get a bit fuzzy here. They wanted a defense against the rapidly rising Sayta. But here on earth where Light is, so Dark is as well. When the Dark and the Light were put together in this unnatural form, it perverted the stone. The stone doesn't work like it was created to, but that doesn't mean it is undesirable. It is very powerful. That power is coveted by the Sayta and is the reason we are being pursued right now."

Going back to the story he continued calmly, "Gwyneth died creating the stone, as did everyone involved. Her family—my ancestors—were brave people. Instead of destroying the stone, not knowing what destruction that could bring, they pledged to safeguard it and keep it from evil purposes. From that time on, Rytra in each generation have tried to protect the stone—with their very lives if necessary."

He looked away for a moment but, before he did, I managed to catch a pained look in his eyes. "I was the one who lost it," he murmured sadly. "The Sayta stole it. They had it enough time to discover that the stone could be useful to them. They discovered that the Dark had so taken over the Light once in the stone, they could now manipulate the stone for their purposes. They managed to turn Rytra into Sayta and send them towards insanity. Because of who we are and our affinity with Light, to be infused with and polluted by Dark can cause insanity. At least it has in all Rytra they have used it on; they were not strong enough to resist its destructive power. The Sayta aren't going insane as you once thought. It was the tainted Rytra, those who had been turned to Dark by the stone and were unable to bear it."

Nathanial plowed on determined to tell it all. "I went after them and retrieved the stone in Mexico. I took it to Seattle because they had just left there: I thought it would be safe there." A heavy sigh broke loose. "Obviously, I was wrong."

We sat in silence for a minute as I let all that he had told me sink in. Everything had finally clicked into place. My breathing slowed slightly. So that was the reason the Rytra had been disappearing! The Sayta had been stealing them away and changing them into Sayta to serve evil. Only it didn't really work well, and instead they went insane. It all made sense now. This long-sought stone could turn Rytra into hybrids so insane they would destroy themselves. The Sayta were obviously planning this fate for me. I was a danger to them, knowing what I did and too stubborn to back off. But what was even worse was that Nathanial was in the middle of this. He had the stone—that stupid stone that he had lied to me about.

Nathanial had lied to me. Right to my face, without showing an ounce of guilt. The thought of it cut into me, digging deeper and deeper until I thought I would cry. How could he? And I thought he trusted me. The sensible part of me told me that he didn't dare tell anyone, but the emotional part couldn't get over the fact that he had lied. The fact that I hadn't noticed hurt almost as much as the fact itself. I had been so stupid.

I reluctantly opened my mouth again. My voice was lifeless. "You lied to me."

Nathanial met my eyes, his own unexpectedly calm. "Yes," he replied smoothly.

"Why?"

He didn't wince as my voice rose. Staring at him through anger-clouded eyes, I wanted to do something. Slapping or punching him as hard as I could was my first choice. Sitting so close in a hidey-hole didn't seem to make that practical.

"I didn't dare let anyone know about it. With only one person knowing, it would be harder for the Sayta to get it. It was the only way, Jo, to do it alone." His eyes, illuminated by moonlight, bored into mine, hard but passionate at the same time. It hit me then: Nathanial was doing all this to protect others. He did not want anyone to be hurt because of something he was responsible for. My anger vanished in an instant. It's kind of funny, how someone can be so angry one minute, and then just tired and sad the next. It was like the anger just drained out of me, and with it went my strength. I went limp against him. I desperately needed rest—there was so much to do.

"I'm not afraid to help you," I whispered. I wasn't. I

wasn't afraid to save him if he needed it. For him, for all the people I loved, I would do anything.

Nathanial chuckled and than gave a sigh. The arms he wrapped around me were gentle. "Then you are an idiot," he said in my ear.

"Perhaps," I agreed softly. "But that doesn't mean I'm wrong."

FIFTEEN

From Ian with Love

Sleep was overtaking me when it suddenly struck me that I hadn't asked the most important question: "Nathanial, where is the stone?"

His arm tightened around my shoulders. "I have it with me," he finally admitted.

"You carry it around with you wherever you go?" I almost yelled. All this time and it had been nearby.

"In a way," he responded cryptically.

I growled. "Nathanial, I swear, if you do not come clean with everything right now, I will gut you like a fish."

He wrinkled his nose. "Thank you for that lovely mental image," he dryly said.

"Nathanial…"

"Right, right, sorry." He sighed. "It's complicated, Jo." My silence was answer enough for him to go on. "Okay. Well, I figured out another use for air. With it, I can create an Otherspace."

"What?"

"An Otherspace. A place outside this dimension, yet always right by my side. Like a traveling bag that can't be seen, yet it's always there, following you around."

"How is that possible?" My voice was almost reverent.

Nathanial shrugged. "I don't know for sure. But, if I

wanted, I could summon the stone, right now. But, as that would cause a… ah… disturbance, I don't think I will."

"So, it lets out a lot of spiritual energy?"

"Yes."

I nodded, falling silent. That was a mistake. As the silence drew us in, holding us close, my ears sharpened. With my eyesight nearly gone (the moon had been hidden by clouds), my other senses were sharpened. Basic human nature. Not to mention the fact that my imagination provided me with all sorts of sounds. It was like I could hear the crackling of the flames from the burning hotel, hear the men screaming all over again. Hear Ian. Hear loving, friendly, kind Ian screaming. Fear, horribly cold and dangerous, seized me. Without even realizing what I was doing, I clutched Nathanial's shirt, huddling closer to his warm body.

"Jo?" His hand gently touched my hair, smoothing it away from my wet face.

"What if… what if he didn't get out? I-I thought I saw… I thought I saw him die. What if Amy didn't get away in time? What if…"

A finger touched my lips, silencing me. "Shh. Don't think about that. It'll only make it worse."

I nodded, trying to do what he said, but my mind would not slow down. "Nathanial, what are we going to do?" My voice was quiet, and I was rather ashamed to hear the note of fear in it and the close-to-sobbing quality of it.

Instead of Nathanial answering, however, a soft breeze blew through the hollow, and on it, there came a voice, "Jo…"

I sat up straight, eyes wide. Next to me, Nathanial was also tense.

"Jo…"

"It's Ian!" I whispered hoarsely.

Nathanial nodded. He could hear it also. He, too, could hear Ian's voice.

"Help me, Jo… I need your help…"

"He's alive!" I sobbed.

Once again, Nathanial's arm tightened. "Tomorrow night, we're going back to the hotel," he murmured into my hair. Before I could protest about not going back right now, he continued: "The Sayta still might be there. We will wait, until tomorrow. If Ian can still use the air to send his voice, he will be able to keep himself alive until then."

I wanted to believe him. There was a desperate need to do so. Because, if I didn't, then I would be admitting that I had just seen my best friend die. And I don't think I could take that. So I didn't say anything else about the vision Scott had shown me or about the blood and the body. It could have been anyone's. Nathanial was right; it was probably just a ruse to get us to go rushing back to the hotel. We simply couldn't do that. So I pushed it all to the back of my mind, where it would stay until I was ready to deal with it. I nodded, wiping away the tears that had escaped. "We'll save him," I said confidently. He pushed me back down against his chest.

"But for now, go to sleep, Jo. We both need rest."

I had to agree.

Before I fell asleep, we decided that we would take turns keeping watch. Nathanial would take the first watch and wake me in four hour's time so he could get some sleep. We would continue to switch off watches until night came once again.

Sleep came but it was filled with mixed dreams of Emily and Ian. Her laugh, her stutter, her smile, ran over and over in my head, haunting me until I awoke. And even then I could practically still hear her.

I opened my eyes, staring at the material of Nathanial's shirt for a few minutes. I miss Emily…my best friend…I don't think I could stand it if I lose Ian also. Not again. I couldn't go through that again.

"Jo?"

I didn't bother to raise my head. It was easier to stare at his shirt than his face. "Tell me he's not dead," I whispered. "Please, Nathanial, tell me."

A hand gently stroked my hair. "Jo…"

Nothing else. That was all he said. No, "I'm sure he's fine." No, "Don't worry; he can take care of himself."

It was because we both knew the truth. We knew that he had a very low chance of survival. Despite hearing his voice, we knew he could have died and his voice could have been a Sayta trick. That thought bore into each of us, tearing us apart.

I felt like a knife was twisting in my heart, shredding it to pieces. The old scars were being torn open, exposed once again. Pain ripping through my soul, tearing me apart piece by piece until there was nothing left but a shattered heap of a person.

Nathanial began to speak in a slow, soft voice.

"Jo, we can't think about those things." His voice was quiet, and his words were for the both of us, not just me.

"We have to believe that he's still alive. If we don't, we'll fall into despair. That can't happen."

I nodded slowly, understanding and agreeing with his words, but also knowing how hard that would be.

"We have a job to do, a duty. Ian tried to stall the Sayta for us, so we could get away. We can't just give up because we mourn him when we don't even know if he's dead. It would make all he did pointless."

Emily's voice echoed in my head, a counterpoint to Nathanial's words. "Right n-now, we m-must go forward," she said when lecturing me about death. "A-afterwards, when we're i-in the c-clear, we can cry and m-mourn. Now, we must l-live for t-t-those that are dead. We must d-do what's right, and go f-forward with dry e-eyes and high heads. Do y-you understand, Jo?"

Yes, Emily, I thought. *Now more than ever. Please give me comfort. Be with me as we go forward into danger. Let me push the sadness away, at least for right now.*

A soft whisper of wind came down into the hollow, brushing against my cheek, wrapping itself around my body for the barest second.

The pain of her death, of the possibility of Ian's death, would never leave. Despite all the years that had passed since Emily's death, I still mourned for her. Now, in a night that never seemed to end, it was in the forefront again, reminding me constantly of her bright eyes and her stutter that I would never hear again. But, for right now, we had a job to do, so the ache is dulled, letting me go forward to do what I must.

SIXTEEN

In Sayta Clutches

The minutes blended together, separated into four hour periods that our lives revolved around. Around noon, Nathanial left our hollow to search for food and water.

It wasn't until midnight that we dared head for Hotel Fairdown. The fear was so thick it clogged my senses, forced me to walk with hesitancy and darting eyes. There were so many possibilities: Ian could be dead, he could be alive but badly injured, we might not even find him, and, worst of all, someone could be waiting for us.

As we walked around the edge of the lake, we were quiet, each dwelling upon our own thoughts. I could tell that Nathanial was preoccupied with pretty much the same things as I was. Without even really realizing what I was doing, I reached out, sliding my hand into his. He looked at me in surprise, but I merely smiled slightly at him. My lips trembled, but I'm not sure if he could tell in the darkness. He relaxed, giving my hand a small squeeze of reassurance. I nodded to myself, calming down considerably. Horrors could, and probably would, be awaiting us at the hotel. We had to be strong, if not for ourselves, then for each other. I thought I could handle that. I thought I could be strong for another. Steeling myself, I forced my emotions away, behind an invisible wall. This was not the place for emotions to rule. That would be our downfall.

Courage is a funny thing. We never think we have it and always strive for it. But when we are in danger, in the thick of things where life was the prize, we find that we do have courage. It is there, hiding inside each of us, just waiting to come out. Cliché and sappy sounding, I know, but it's true. As we walked to the hotel, I found that little reserve of courage in the back of my heart, strong and silent. No matter what, I thought I would be able to face my challenges. They might break me, but at least I had the satisfaction of knowing that I faced them despite the fear gnawing at my insides, waiting to take over if courage failed.

The hotel stank of the Dark. Everything was cloaked in Dark. We hesitated at the edge, unwilling to step into it. I was the first to move, forcing my feet forward. When the Dark came over me, it wasn't pleasant, but it was manageable. Nathanial shuddered visibly as he followed.

Ash crumbled beneath our feet. Retrieving my hand from Nathanial's, I bent down, absently running my fingers lightly over the fine-grained black dust. It was cool to the touch and rough. The hotel, burned and deteriorated, rose before us, a dark testimony to the reason we were here. The reason we fought for survival against the Sayta. A headstone, if you will.

The moonlight fell upon it, casting half of it into shadows. Silvery moonlight played across the lake, barely penetrating the trees. Under it, I didn't know whether I felt better for the light or more exposed. I shifted nervously, dreading to enter the collapsed building. Nathanial, without a single glance in my direction, started forward. Scowling slightly at his demeanor, I followed.

"Jo?" he whispered as we moved among the burnt stone and charred pieces of wood, searching for something, anything.

"Mm?"

"I'm sorry."

I glanced at him, not really knowing what to think. "For what?" I whispered. But I never even had the time to find out.

From our left side, where everything was hidden in shadows, there came the sound of clapping.

We spun, tense and wide-eyed. Boots crunched on the remains of the stone, leaving imprints in the ash. Scott, his eyes gleaming with cunning and dark amusement, stepped out of the shadows that had cloaked him. Behind him were other Sayta, laughing at Nathanial and me, and our foolishness. I silently called for the Light. This is not good.

"Now, now, Josephine," scolded Scott lightly. "Don't do anything rash." His teeth glittered in the weak light, like some predator.

I glared, jaw clenched tightly. "You were here all along, weren't you?" I asked in a deadly soft voice that shook with rage. "You used the Dark to cloak you. You knew we would come back."

Scott smirked, leaning against a pillar of stone, arms crossed lazily over his chest. "Yes, you are right, as usual, my dear." He chuckled, rather sinisterly. "You are so predictable, Josephine. I knew you would come back, searching for your beloved Ian."

My blood froze. "What did you do to him?"

The smirk broadened. "We set fire to the hotel," he

drawled, obviously enjoying my suffering. "What do you think happened to him?"

"No... We heard his voice! There is still the chance that he's alive!" No. Please...!

Scott laughed. "Yes. Of course you heard him. After all, it was my men who used the last bit of his soul to project his voice on the wind." My heart nearly stopped. I had thought something seemed wrong; now, unfortunately, I knew I was right. Ian wouldn't risk calling for help via air, not when the Sayta were nearby. His glittering eyes were alight with perverse amusement. "He's dead, Jo. He was hurt badly by the fire, but still alive when I got here. He killed many of the Sayta, as I'm sure you'll be pleased to know." A slight frown crept onto his face, but it was replaced by a despicable smirk a second later. "I thrust the knife into his heart myself, Jo. I watched him die."

My hands clenched into fists. "NO!" I screamed aloud, tears burning in my eyes. But I would not let them fall. I would not give Scott the satisfaction of seeing me cry.

"Yes, Jo. He's dead."

N-no... he can't be dead... I took a breath. There was no point in dwelling on the fact, not now. I have to be strong. For Ian. The coldness of resolve settled on my shoulders like a cloak. Looking at Scott, I stuck my hands on my hips, assuming the most defiant pose I could muster.

"What are you, Scotty boy?" I shouted. "You are not Sayta."

"No," Scott agreed with a little nod of his head. "I am a normal human being."

Gibes were on the tip of my tongue, but this was not a time to provoke him. I couldn't keep all of the sarcasm out of my voice, however. "So, since you are merely a non-magical human gone evil, how did you use Rytra powers?"

Scott nodded, obviously pleased. "Well done. I wondered if you would ask me that. Well, you see, I have a little magical artifact also." Reaching into his pocket, he withdrew a plain pocket watch. It twirled on its gold chain, reflecting the moonlight in a dull bronze color. "It enables me to use Rytra powers. It's been filled with the power of your dearest, detestable Light." The ever-annoying smirk was back. "Useful, no?"

Grudgingly, I had to admit it was. "So, Scott; what are you going to do with us?"

I stole a glance at Nathanial. He had been silent this whole time, one hand in his pocket. I wondered if his stone was there, wondered if he had summoned it, and then dismissed the idea. We would have felt the energy. He was waiting, biding his time, content to let Scott and I banter.

Scott pushed himself off the wall with one shoulder. "Another good question," he murmured, starting to walk towards us. I tensed up again, readying myself for a fight. "You see, I have an opportunity here. I have two perfectly good Rytra, right in front of my nose, and the owner of the stone, of course." His grin widened, and I was reminded of a dangerous wild cat. "I think it would be a large blow indeed if RODD's top Rytra were to fall and become a Sayta."

"In your dreams, buddy boy."

He raised his hand, and the Sayta gathered behind him began to stream forward, darkness pouring from their hands. Nathanial snapped up a barrier, preparing to block their attacks while I drew on the power of the elements to return strike.

"Oh, but didn't I tell you?" Scott's taunting voice rose over the sounds of the Sayta. "In this world, in my domain, my dreams are quite real."

I rolled my eyes. "Dreams? Yeah right! Nightmares are more like it!" I parried a strike, slipped under the Sayta's defenses, and struck with a sword of light that pierced him through and through. His scream rose in the night air, disturbing the relative stillness of the surrounding woods.

There was a cry beside me, and I looked without thinking. Nathanial was on one knee, holding his side. Blood leaked between his fingers, gently dripping down to stain his clothes and the grayness of the stone beside him. Just for an instant, his eyes caught and held mine. Everything and nothing seemed to radiate from those eyes, the eyes that had first caught my attention so long ago. But, the one thing that I really noticed, the one thing that seemed to strike my soul, was the single sentence those eyes seemed to impart.

"I'm sorry."

There were those words again. And at the sight of those sorrowful eyes, a tiny crack appeared in the ice, spider webbing quickly into a thousand of other cracks. *How does he manage to destroy all my barriers and get into my heart?* I asked myself. *How does he manage to reduce my legs to jelly with a single look?*

How does he manage to make me fall in love with him without even trying?

Even in this place, this Dark place with the coppery smell of blood rising on the night wind, that pang of love was still inside me. I thought that I would be able to forget that emotion, too, at least for a little while. But no. It seemed that when the emotion was strong enough, nothing could suppress it.

I took a step closer to Nathanial, intending to protect him and heal him so he could go on fighting, but it just wasn't to be.

The only warning I had was the slight widening of Nathanial's eyes, the note of alarm that flickered quickly through him.

I spun, starting to raise a barrier of air, hoping against hope that I wasn't too slow.

Hope, and luck, were not with me. It seemed like they never had been.

I barely caught a glimpse of the throng of Sayta. Then pain. Pain exploding through my body, tearing me slowly apart. If I could have, I would have screamed. But it seemed like I could make no move whatsoever. It was as if my muscles were frozen, locked in place. Darkness. That was all there seemed to be. Darkness sweeping over me, consuming me, bringing me down into an inescapable pool.

It obliterated everything, and I remembered no more.

I woke slowly, painfully. My head hurt worse than I thought possible, and it was a few moments before I could even open my eyes. I could feel something restraining me—a binding—a supernatural bond that a Rytra or Sayta puts on their prisoners to keep them from using their powers. It usually causes intense discomfort, and it was no different with me. I wanted nothing more than to escape, to crawl out of my skin so I couldn't feel the binding, but that was beyond impossible. I continued to stay still for a moment longer, simply breathing deeply to try and keep myself in check. Then, slowly, I opened my eyes to see where I was.

The room was rather lavishly furnished, with large, red plush armchairs scattered around. A dark cherry wood desk was in front of the large window, which was covered in thick red drapes. The carpet was soft and also red. All the red reminded me of blood: Emily's, Ian's—and now Nathanial's. I tried to look anywhere but at the red. Book-cases completely covered one wall, and more stood on either side of the roaring fireplace. All other light was provided by lamps, placed around the room on small tables. In front of the fire, sitting comfortably in a chair, was Scott. I shifted, furious, wanting nothing more than to rip him apart. He must have heard my movement, for he turned, fingers laced together and a smug smile on his face.

"Hello, Josephine," he practically purred.

I didn't bother with any pleasantries. Slowly, trying not to wince, I raised myself into a sitting position, albeit an uncomfortable one.

I looked up at him. "Where's Nathanial?"

"Is that all you can say? Shouldn't you be begging me for mercy? Or something like that, in any case."

"I'd rather die."

"That can be arranged."

I snorted, laughing haughtily. "You won't kill me. You want me to be a Sayta."

Scott looked at me curiously, eyes narrowing a bit. "How do you know I haven't changed my mind?"

"I think I know you well enough for that. You wouldn't

give up a valuable—let's see, how shall we label me? Ah yes, specimen will do. You wouldn't give up a valuable specimen like me. And besides, wouldn't you have killed me while I was unconscious if you wanted to be rid of me?"

Scott inclined his head slightly. "Very nicely thought through."

Most of my confidence was feigned. In fact, I was kind of shocked at myself for being so bold and insolent. Hostages weren't supposed to goad their captors, after all. But I just couldn't help it. My tongue would not be still. Some part of me wanted to destroy Scott completely. Since I obviously could not do it with physical actions, words would have to suffice.

Scott leaned forward, holding my gaze with his own. "You are in my clutches, Josephine," he said softly. His voice was pitched low and a shiver went through me, despite my best effort to stop it. He grinned slightly, eyes glittering with something that truly scared me. "I can do whatever I want with you."

No! I wouldn't let him do anything to me—or Nathanial. I started to build up power, not thinking clearly, ignoring the warning pain as the binding tightened, but the next moment I was lying on my side, blood trickling from my mouth and nose.

"That hurt," I protested thickly, struggling back up into my sitting position.

Scott loomed above me, tall and powerful. He glared down, and for the first time, despite his boyish appearance he looked dangerous. Very dangerous. It scared me, but I forced the fear deep inside, where I wouldn't feel it for now. Now was not the time for fear. And I wouldn't give Scott the pleasure of seeing me tremble.

"Really?" he said gratingly. "I wonder why?"

"No clue."

He twitched, his eyes flickering with anger. "Your remarks are quickly beginning to annoy me," he warned in a deadly voice.

To prevent myself from saying something that would make him go over the edge (and since it's me, I most certainly would), I demanded instead, "Where's Nathanial? I want to see him."

Scott sneered. "Hostages have no right to make demands."

I glowered at him.

He sighed. "Fine." He smirked a little. "I suppose it'll help him to be more cooperative if he sees that you're still alive."

Scott opened the door, and I saw two Sayta standing guard. Scott murmured something to one, and the guard immediately went off, leaving the remaining one alone. Returning to the room, Scott took out a knife. It gleamed in the lamplight, and a little bit of uneasiness started to well up within me.

He moved behind me, and I twisted, trying to see what he was doing. To my ultimate shock, he cut my rope bonds but left the binding in place. I must have been staring, because his mouth twisted wryly.

"I don't think Nathanial will be very cooperative when he sees you trussed up like a goose."

I sat there, massaging my wrists, eyes locked on the door. When at last it opened, I was on my feet before Nathanial entered the room. He was dirty and looked exhausted. He was limping heavily, one hand clutching his side; his clothes were blood-splattered. He staggered forward, weary but determined. I reached him before he reached me and wrapped my arms around him to help support him.

He drew me away gently, his eyes flickering over my person. "You okay?" he asked. His voice was rough.

I smiled a little. "Yeah. You, however, are a mess."

He smiled back, although it did not reach his eyes. "Still blunt as always, I see."

"Why wouldn't I be?"

His eyes never once left mine. Just as before, amid the destruction of the hotel, his eyes seemed to speak to me. "It's all right," they said. "I won't let them hurt you."

"That's not what I'm afraid of," I murmured, reaching up to touch his cheek. "Don't do anything foolish, all right? I'm stronger than I look."

"I know," he whispered hoarsely.

"Well, as touching as this reunion is, I'm afraid I must interrupt," Scott said, walking toward us.

The next moment, strong arms wrapped around my waist and I was pulled tightly against the body of a huge Sayta. I struggled, but the knife at my throat effectively stilled me. Sharp metal gently bit into soft flesh, causing little dots of red to bead up. Nathanial growled but didn't move. He understood the message as I did.

"I think we'll be able to strike a deal," Scott said, that smug look once more in place. "Now, Nathanial. Hand over the stone, and I will not harm your girlfriend."

I snorted. "Using the stone against me isn't hurting me?"

Scott chuckled. "Well, I suppose you could look at it like

that. Of course, there is no guarantee that it'll actually hurt you. You might walk away unscathed." He turned back to Nathanial. "Here's the deal. Once we get to a special, designated area, you will hand over the stone, or Josephine will be hurt very badly. Do you really want to put her through both physical and mental torture?"

Nathanial hesitated, gripped by indecision. "Don't be a fool!" I snapped, ignoring the warning prick of the knife. "I'll be fine. I can handle my nightmares just fine!"

"Really?" Scott said unbelievingly. "I highly doubt that. So, Nathanial, what will your decision be?"

"Don't!" I screamed.

Nathanial looked at me… and I knew in that instant that he would do what Scott said. Everything was lost, and there was nothing I could do about it.

"You have a deal," Nathanial said, his voice stony. "But you'd better hold up your end of the bargain."

There was no reply. Several Sayta took him out of the room. I was led out next. At last I was deposited in a bedroom. The double bed was plain with a dark blue comforter on it. There was only a single, small window with metal bars on it. The door closed as my guard left, clicking shut as it was locked.

Staring at the hard oak floor, I felt like all hope was undeniably gone.

SEVENTEEN

Upon Gray Stones

I didn't sleep much, of course. Most of the night I passed by crying into my pillow. And when I finally did fall asleep, one of the Sayta woke me up what seemed like a minute later. I stared blankly at him for a moment, then sighed and swung my legs over the side of the bed. We remained silent as he led me down the hall, past other bedrooms, into a large, empty room. Scott was there, tapping his fingers impatiently on his arm. Nathanial stood nearby, wrists bound behind his back, his head held up high.

"Finally," snapped Scott on my arrival.

He was twitching, shifting from foot to foot, his temper high. In other words, he was scared. If the situation had been any different, it would have been amusing to watch him worry. But, seeing as there literally was no hope for anything, not even his antics could amuse me.

"A transportation?" I balked, frowning as I saw what was about to happen. "But how? We use air to transport. You're Sayta... kind of."

He rolled his eyes. "I can still pose as a Rytra, Josephine. I can still use the air, and other elements of Light, no matter how much it detests me to do so. Didn't I prove that when I nearly managed to kill you with our last transportation?"

So it had been his fault! I should have known. In a corner

of my mind, I probably did. I didn't say anything else as the transportation began. I leaned slightly against Nathanial, taking comfort in his presence. My hands had been bound; otherwise I would have literally clung to him.

I couldn't say where we ended up. I had never been there before. It was a desolate place, to say the least. Everything was gray stone. I shivered slightly at that sight, wanting nothing more than to get off the stone. It reminded me too much of the reason we were all here. Who knew? Maybe "the stone" itself was from this very patch of rock. It ranged from dark, storm-cloud gray to light blue-gray. There was nothing around us for miles. We were on a cliff, which dropped off rather sharply into the ocean. The waves pounded against the cliff, heavy and unrelenting, a steady cadence. Throwing my head back, I examined the sky. Dark, rolling masses of clouds were gathering, promising rain. Why did it always seem to be raining no matter where I was?

To my surprise, we were not alone. Five people were waiting for us. Some were scowling, others seemed curious, and one just looked bored. I noticed a girl with blue eyes who bounced on the balls of her feet eagerly.

The last man who caught my attention wasn't very tall; maybe five feet, six inches. He had shoulder-length pure white hair, and one of his eyes was covered with a milky sheen. His other eye was black, gleaming with intelligence. Seeing us, his impatient scowl turned into a deep smile that curled his thin lips upwards.

Upon reaching the white-haired man, all the Sayta bowed, Scott the lowest. "The girl and the keeper of the stone, as you requested, sir," he said reverently.

Whitey smiled and nodded. He came forward, reaching out to grab my chin. I tried to jerk it angrily out of his grasp, but his hold was like iron. "Now, now," he murmured, his voice deep and cold. "Don't fight, my little prize."

I went stiff with shock. I knew that voice! But from where? It took me nearly a full minute to figure it out. I nearly choked as the realization hit me. "You!" I cried. "You're the one that was on the phone when we were impersonating Joe Year!"

Whitey chuckled. "My, we do have a memory, don't we?"

"Talking of yourself in the royal plural?" I taunted, unable to help myself.

I winced slightly, waiting for the expected smack. It never came, however. Whitey just kept on smiling, that cold look in his eye scaring me more and more. "My name is Pierce Court. I run this little operation. You know, getting the stone and all. And you, of course. I have had my eye on you for quite some time now, Josephine Whitwalker. You are the main reason the Rytra have not totally crumpled under Sayta rule. With you gone, there will be little holding them up."

"Pierce Court," I repeated, musing over the name. I had never heard it before. "An alias?" I questioned.

"Maybe," Court replied mysteriously. He nodded to Scott, who signaled to the man holding me. He dragged me forward until a circle of Sayta had closed around me and Nathanial.

"All right," Court said. "Give me the stone—NOW!"

A knife was held to my throat. I was almost getting used to it. I didn't expect the knife to suddenly dip, however, drawing blood as it was lightly dragged down to right above my heart. I flinched, struggling to ignore the red-hot pain.

Nathanial, his eyes dark, angry, and sorrowful, made a soft noise in his throat. Then he held out his hand. It began to glow, dimly at first, then with more power. I watched, transfixed, as something appeared in the air right above his hand. A minute later, the bright light faded, and an object dropped into his palm. The gray stone. The plain stone that literally gave off waves of power. I shivered, trying to back away from it.

The Sayta grinned, their smiles mirroring one another. Court grasped the stone quickly. He held it up, examining it in the weak light. He began to laugh slowly, a menacing cackle that sent shivers up my spine.

Still grinning, Court turned to face me. "Are you ready, Josephine Whitwalker?" he asked. "Are you ready to become one of us?"

"That's a rhetorical question, correct?" I muttered sardonically in reply. Apparently the terror gripping me did not slow my tongue. The fear inside me was like a snake, coiling around my insides, squeezing me to death. My breathing was quickening, my chest rising and falling rapidly. I wanted to calm down, but it was impossible. This was it. I was afraid. So terribly afraid.

The Sayta holding me let go, stepping away. A moment later, the vile touch of Sayta Dark fell over me, rooting me to one spot. Compared to this, a binding was nothing. A binding didn't have direct Dark in it, after all, while this did. A chilly wind picked up, whirling around us like a ghostly dance for the lost. Looking up through whirling tendrils of my hair, I spotted Nathanial, being held much like I was. He looked terrified for me. Catching my eyes, he did something I wasn't expecting: he nodded, as if to assure me that everything would be okay.

Then there was a burst of power that obliterated everything but itself. I stared in horrid fascination at the winding power coming for me. I tried to brace myself for it, but there was no time. It hit me squarely in the chest, spreading out to cover my entire body. I screamed, but it was drowned out by the sudden crescendo of the wind, heightened by the power. It was burgeoning through me, sinking past my skin to embed itself into every fiber of my being.

Then the pain came. It erupted inside of me, making me cry out again. It was worse than anything I could think of. It seemed like the power was trying to destroy me, destroy the very soul of my being. I was being recreated into something else. Darkness was seeping over me. But it wasn't the darkness of unconsciousness. Rather it was the Dark of the Sayta. It was entering me, curling up like some evil creature in my soul. It was trying to take over everything in me, push out all the Light in my being.

No! I silently screamed. I need the Light! I whimpered. I could withstand this... I thought blearily. But... but it hurts! It hurts so much! How can I keep both the Dark and the Light inside of me? Oh, please, someone... someone... Help me!

Time faded. I don't know how long I was there, feeling the Dark and the Light battling for supremacy inside of me. Then... quite suddenly, it subsided. They were there, side-by-side, both inside of me. And I was alive, judging from the amount of leftover pain that I was still going through.

I dared to open my eyes. I found myself slumped in the hold the Sayta had created around me. I didn't even have the strength to hold myself up. The Sayta all had looks of joy on their faces, glancing repeatedly over at Court who still held the stone. His eyes were large and wild, giving him the accurate impression of being a madman. When the binding and hold were taken away, I collapsed to my hands and knees, head down, panting heavily. My limbs convulsed slightly from the pain.

Footsteps. I didn't bother looking up, but continued to sit there and stare at the stone. Strong hands grabbed me, hauling me up. I flopped uselessly, all my strength long gone.

"Well, you're alive," Court murmured. He sounded rather weary himself, but absurdly pleased. "And I can sense Sayta power in you." He turned to look at someone behind him. "Hannah, confirm her power."

The curious girl who had been bouncing before came up and kneeled beside me. She reached out, smiling, expecting only Sayta power.

A moment later she gave a scream of shock, falling away from me.

"What?" snapped Court. I raised tired eyes to find Hannah staring at me as if I had grown an extra head or two.

"She-she is still a R-Rytra!" she wailed, stuttered a bit.

"What?" Court demanded in horror and fury. "But that's not possible!" He whirled angrily on Nathanial. "You! This is all your fault! Your stone malfunctioned!"

I opened my mouth to tell him that it wasn't Nathanial's

fault, actually, that I knew I was the one that could withstand both Dark and Light living inside of me. The words wouldn't come, however, and my tongue remained still.

Court moved forward. Darkness poured off him, twining together to form a sword-like object. It rushed forward, undeterred by the still-strong wind, going forward to plunge into Nathanial's chest.

"NO!"

The drawn-out word tore itself from my throat painfully. I struggled forward to my knees; one hand desperately outstretched as if somehow I could reach out and bring Nathanial to me.

I watched as if in slow-motion as Nathanial staggered, blood flecking his lips, dripping from the gaping wound in his chest. His skin went from pale to white in less than a second. His eyes grew wide with shock, and he tried to stem the heavy flow of blood. The darkness retreated, leaving the wound exposed to the salty air. Around the edges of it, the skin was black as death itself, a mark left from the dark sword. Nathanial staggered back, to the edge of the cliff. A look of surprise crossed his beautiful, lined face. He was falling backwards, all black and red and white skin.

Then he was gone, simply gone.

EIGHTEEN

New Powers

No. It just couldn't be. He couldn't be dead. Not him too. Not Nathanial too! I was sobbing, my whole body shaking, and I didn't care. I struggled to get to my feet. That small act seemed to sap my strength, and I nearly fell back to the earth. Locking my knees, I forced myself to continue standing. Hannah glanced at me but seemed too shocked to try to restrain me. Stupid girl.

No...!

My head felt fuzzy, and it was hard to think straight. I staggered, nearly falling, to the cliff side, where Court still stood. He glanced at me, his eyes more wild than ever. I stared right back at him, silent now. I raised a hand, then brought it slashing down, summoning fire without thinking. It was just so easy. It was there, at my fingertips, just waiting for me to use it. Court was so surprised that he barely managed to get a shield up. It was weak, however, and the fire burned right through it. He screamed, falling backwards, uselessly attempting to put the fire out.

There were cries from the others as they rushed forward. They were going to restrain me! I couldn't let that happen. I looked over the cliff to the thrashing waves. I sent out a rush of healing water, silently bidding it: keep Nathanial alive.

If he was still alive, that is.

Closing my eyes, I let the air sweep over me, telling it to take me to Seattle, Dyose's office. Darkness engulfed me for a minute, pierced every now and then by a bright light of something. Then, with a heavy thunk, I hit the floor of my destination.

Opening my eyes warily, I was comforted by the familiar surroundings of my boss's office. There was a cry of shock from behind me, and I turned to face Dyose. He looked exhausted, almost as tired as I felt. He wore no tie for once, and the collar of his shirt was unbuttoned. I burst into tears. I would have thought that I had no more tears left in me, but apparently not. I slipped to my knees, crying my heart out.

Dyose knelt beside me, placing one hand on my shoulder. He was saying something, asking something, but I couldn't distinguish the words. "I couldn't save them," I sobbed, burying my head in my hands.

I was falling forward, pain and exhaustion crashing over me like a tidal wave. Strong hands grabbed me, preventing me from face-planting. Dyose's voice rose, calling my name, but I was unable to respond.

I couldn't... save... them...

He was the same age as me, but his powers had been discovered later than mine. He was hopelessly untrained, and unless something was done, he might be consumed by his powers. I was chosen to teach him. Maybe they were hoping I would manage to make friends with him, become my old self again. Emily was gone, and since her death, I hadn't made any good friends. I hadn't been myself, and my abilities had languished because of it. He was alone, too, despite the

fact that he was much more likable than I. Maybe they were hoping
we would be good for each other and that would be good for RODD.

He wasn't shy. From our first meeting, when we met in my little
apartment, he didn't hold back.

Smiling, he stuck out his hand for me to shake. "I'm Ian
McKinley, but you can call me Ian."

"Josephine Whitwalker," I replied, a little uneasily.

"All right then, Jo, shall we get crackin'?"

His tone, the manner in which he spoke, was slightly surprising,
but wonderfully refreshing. That first afternoon, I found myself
actually relaxing. I was laughing, and talking freely, as I struggled
to guide him through the trials that all Rytra go through.

In time, he became my best friend. He didn't take Emily's place,
of course. No one could do that. He merely stood alongside her. If
she had still been alive, I think they would have gotten along
wonderfully. He was the one who saw me laugh, and cry, and was
always there for me.

The thought he might leave me was not conceivable.

I opened my eyes slowly, staring at nothing. Why must I
think of him, so soon?

"You awake?"

I nodded, not looking at Dyose. "Where am I?" I asked.
My tone was emotionless, despite the hundreds of emotions
swirling in me.

"My house," Dyose replied. He hesitated, obviously not
knowing whether or not to ask. "What happened,
Whitwalker?" he finally asked.

I closed my eyes. Despite this, tears began to trickle down. "They're dead."

"Who are?"

"Ian. Maybe Nathanial. I don't know if I managed to save him or not."

"Whitwalker." Dyose reached out, laying his hand on my shoulder once more. "What happened? Why... why do you feel like a Sayta and a Rytra at the same time?" He crossed himself as he said it.

So I explained everything. Dyose knew some of it already, from the phone call from Amy, but he let me go on. He just sat there, eyes closed as he listened, chin propped up in his hands. When I was finished, my boss sat there, processing the information for a few minutes. He didn't look disgusted or revolted by the fact that I was part Sayta now, but he didn't exactly look happy either.

"All right," he said at last. "So, Nathanial might still be alive?"

"Yes."

"Then the first thing we need to do is go get him. Do you know where you were?"

I stared at him, unable to believe what I was hearing. "S-sir? Are you serious?"

Dyose looked at me calmly. "Do I normally joke around?"

"No... but..."

"But what, Whitwalker?" he demanded. "What else do you propose we do? Go off and find Scott and Court, defeat them, and get the stone? Yes, we will do that, but not right now. We need to gather our strength, find our enemies, and proceed with caution."

"Sir, I agree wholeheartedly with the finding-Nathanial

part. But we also need to get the stone now! Do you know how many Sayta that Scott and Court—if he's still alive—will have by the time we're ready to face them?"

He didn't say anything else, but his look clearly told me not to question him. Dyose rose. "Help yourself to anything in the kitchen; I'm going out." As he reached the door, he hesitated, looking back at me. "And don't even think about leaving." He obviously thought that, since he was still my boss, I would faithfully obey his orders.

As soon as he was gone, after I heard his car roar off, I got up. I was a little shaky, but after walking through his house until the weakness disappeared, I felt as good as ever. It was strange, but exhilarating at the same time. I guess my new powers strengthened me. The thought wasn't entirely unpleasant.

What was unpleasant, however, was the knowledge that I was now a Sayta. That thought frightened me a bit, but knowing that I was still a Rytra also, and that would help control the Dark powers now in me, reassured me. I could feel the Dark, but it wasn't as revolting as it once had been. And I could feel the other elements now, just out of range, waiting for my call. I was slightly surprised at how well I was taking all this.

Walking into Dyose's bathroom, I stepped into the shower. Showers were great places to think. They helped clear one's head. And as I stood there letting warm water run over me, I pondered my new dual nature. How could it be? I was a servant of Light; Darkness was my worst enemy. So how could I be like this and yet feel comfortable?

It is human nature to walk in the Dark. We are sinners,

even the Rytra; it is part of our being. Sometimes the Dark overcomes people. Other times, no matter how strong the Dark, we can withstand it. God had made me like that; had given me the ability to withstand the Dark. I would be able to live with the Dark in me, but not be controlled by it. Despite everything that had happened—everything that was happening—I smiled. And although no one living could protect me, I felt safe.

After basking in the warm water for a while, I reluctantly got out. Dressed in a towel and hoping that Dyose didn't happen to come back soon, I murmured a quick request to my elemental friends. They obediently washed and dried my clothes. I slid back into them, the cloth gentle and warm against my skin. Finger-combing my damp hair, I jammed my feet back into my shoes and wandered into the kitchen area.

Making myself a quick turkey sandwich, I thought about the plan I had come up with in the bathroom. "Get the elements to take me back to the coast, find Nathanial, then go after Scott and Court," I murmured to myself. "Right." I glanced around Dyose's house, shaking my head a little. "I know. You told me to wait here. But, you see, sir, I just can't. I can't just stand by, obeying your orders, when I know I'm right. For once," I added dryly.

I rubbed my hands together. "Right, guys," I murmured to the elements. They stirred, getting ready to obey my orders. "Let's go to Aunt Penny's." I bent my will to them, ordering them to take me there. The winds of transportation immediately engulfed me. A few minutes later, I was dumped unceremoniously on the dark green front lawn. Hauling my aching body up, I looked at the large white house towering above me. Not wasting any time, I jogged up the steps, knocking harshly on the door a few times before turning the knob. It was unlocked, so I stepped it.

"Hello?" I called experimentally. "Aunt Penny? Mum? Amy?"

"Jo!"

The next minute, I was engulfed in a sea of strong, groping arms. My mother and Amy were hugging me tightly at the same time, both sobbing like there was no tomorrow. I gently pushed the two women away. "Sorry, I need to breathe," I panted, holding my creaking ribs.

Amy stepped back and looked over me, eyes flickering rapidly. "So," she murmured after a long moment of silence. "They managed to do it, didn't they? But—you're still Rytra."

I explained everything that had happened, and Amy, in turn, told me that Dyose and RODD in Seattle were preparing to move. I didn't mention that Dyose wasn't all together too happy with me.

"What are you going to do, Josephine?" my mother asked calmly.

I looked at her, and knew that no matter what, she would support my decision. "I'm going to save Nathanial, then go after Court and Scott," I replied firmly.

"Do you want me to come with you?" Amy asked. "I'm ready and willing if you do."

I shook my head. "Sorry, Amy, but no. I'm going to need you to take care of Nathanial when I bring him back here."

"Why don't you take him to Dyose? There will be more people to heal him."

I shook my head again. "No. Dyose won't let me go if I go

back. He's rather afraid of my new powers, I think. I have to go after Court and Scott. For Ian; for Nathanial; for everyone who has suffered under them. I can't let Dyose handle everything. He just doesn't understand." I chuckled weakly. "I don't even know if I understand. But it's something I'm going to do, whether I have his permission or not."

Amy smiled gently. "All right. Just be careful, okay?"

"I promise." Then, closing my eyes, I ordered the air to take me to the cliff side where Nathanial disappeared.

There were no signs of life on the rocky plain, thankfully. The Sayta were gone, but a faint trace of power and death still lingered around the place. I stood still for a moment, gathering my wits, before silently calling the air and ordering it to take me down the cliff. It obeyed, forming an invisible but solid moving platform beneath me. The waves lapped at the bottom of the solid air, easily seen and disturbing. Looking up, I gulped a little, finally and fully appreciating just how high the cliff was. I scanned its face, looking for a small pocket, a cave. I found one right near the waves. A few tall rocks led the way to it like a pathway. Directing the air to the cave, I left the ocean behind me and entered the dark abyss of the enclosure.

It was pitch black inside, with only the weak sunlight outside illuminating a few feet. I ordered a small but strong light to brighten my way. Dismissing the air I had called, I lifted the light up to bring the whole place into my sight.

The rock beneath me was the same, hard gray stone as above, but this was moist and salty from the sea. The floor sloped steeply up, the end of it rising above the point of high tide. I scrabbled upwards, the hard purchase of the rock making it easy. At the top, lying on his back with his eyes closed was Nathanial.

His breathing was shallow and too slow, but at least he was breathing. His chest was an absolute mess, torn and bloodied and blackened. Only the water converging upon it kept him alive. I ran up to him, falling to my knees, and placed both my hands over the ghastly wound. "Heal," I whispered. More water came, obeying my call, and whirled around him. I don't know how long I kept at it. I steadily continued to struggle to heal him until he was stable. Normally I wasn't the greatest at healing, despite it being the talent first discovered. But now, tired and mentally exhausted as I was, it took all the longer to try and close the wound.

When I was finished exhaustion hit me, but I stubbornly shook it off. Checking Nathanial's pulse, I breathed a sigh of relief to find that it was much stronger than it had been. Wrapping my arms around him as tightly as I dared, I told the air to take us home.

I knocked on the door, waiting until I heard Amy say, "Come in."

In the brightly lit room, my eyes immediately went to Nathanial. He lay, still and silent on the single bed. His skin was sickly pale, and he hadn't woken up yet.

"How is he?" I whispered, even though there was no real need to.

Amy smiled sadly, sponging off his forehead. "He's not in the best condition, Jo. I don't know if he'll make it."

The pain entered my heart again, but I didn't cry. I think all of my tears were gone, spent earlier. "But there's a chance," I murmured.

Amy nodded. "There's always a chance. If his will to live is strong enough, I'm sure he'll pull through. We're all praying for him."

I nodded, wishing there was something more we could do. The idea struck me so suddenly I gasped excitedly. "Amy, if the watch can give Rytra powers to someone like Scott, who's not a Rytra, wouldn't it amplify a real Rytra's powers?"

Amy paused, looked at me, and began to grin.

I awoke surprisingly well rested. After soaking in the shower, I dressed completely in black: shirt, pants, and my useful black boots. Leaving the room, I entered the kitchen where everyone was gathered. Even Aunt Penny was there. She was six years older than my mum, with plenty of wrinkles and steel gray hair. Everyone looked up at my entrance, and a kind of ominous silence fell. I smiled or at least attempted to and said, "Well, I guess I'll be going now."

They didn't even try to dissuade me, knowing this was the only course of action.

Although I wished I could just walk past Nathanial's room—it would probably be easier—I was weak, and stopped. I went in, crouching down by his bedside. Reaching out, I ran my fingers over his skin. It was smooth and cold, like marble. A marble statue of a man. Looking at him, sleeping apparently peacefully, I was filled with new determination. "Don't worry," I murmured into his deaf ears. "I'll be back. And I'll have that watch with me. No matter what." I gently kissed his cheek. The skin was deathly cold to my lips, but I didn't pull away immediately. "I won't let you die, you know. I'm kind of stubborn that way."

Rising, I left the room, not looking back once.

NINETEEN

Out of Court

Once in a safe, secluded place, I summoned the elements to take me to the house in the woods where I had been kept captive by Scott. A few minutes later, I found myself on the front porch of the old house. I could tell from the landscape I was back in England, although I had no idea exactly where. No one seemed to be around, so my slip-up hadn't cost me anything except a few brown hairs now gray. I breathed a sigh of relief. Eyes wide open, making sure that I was holding no power whatsoever that could be detected by Sayta, I crept to the back of the house. There was a window near my height; rising on my tiptoes, I looked over the sill. The room I saw was the sitting room Scott had been in before. The drapes were partially pulled back, so I could only make out a little bit of the room. I didn't see anyone. Luckily or unluckily, I'm not quite sure.

Still not completely sure what in the world I was doing, I ran my hands over the window, digging my nails into the bottom. Casting vigilant glances around me, I pulled upwards with all my strength. The window didn't open. I noticed the latch in the middle of it. Never letting up my lookout, I reached into my boot and withdrew a small, incredibly sharp knife. Inserting it into the crack, I carefully lifted it up slowly, so not to make any excess noise. Then I gave the window a little push. It was old so it creaked softly. I winced, freezing in place, waiting with baited breath for someone to find me out. When no one did, I dared to breathe again, which was a good thing in the long run. Still moving as if in slow motion, I opened the window enough to slip through. Once in I closed it, repositioning the drapes into what I hoped they were like before I snuck in.

Then the door to the room burst open and everything was wreathed in flames.

I acted on instinct. Throwing up a shield, I made it fire-proof, and only then concentrated on who had entered the room. I blew out a breath, feeling a strange urge to chuckle. It was the two Sayta who had guarded Nathanial and me—the ones who constantly felt the need to hold a knife to my neck.

"What, startled?" the exceptionally large Sayta taunted. "Didja actually think that the desk—that the room—would be left unguarded? Boss thought you might come back, to get the stone an' all. Both desk and room was covered with sensors." He nudged the other, who was concentrating wholly on the fire he was controlling. "We were waitin' for you."

The next moment the fire was all the brighter, all the stronger, and all the more power-consuming. "You are so unprofessional," I chided. "Using so much power and all. By doing that, you leave yourselves rather open."

Not wasting any more time on useless, if amusing, conversation, I raised my hand, palm up. Light and air gathered there, melding together to form a white-gray, slightly opaque, orb. I let the shield disappear, calling to the fire raging around me at the same time. It had to be timed precisely or else I could be killed. Fortunately, my precision was top-notch. The fire gathered around my other hand, forming a halo-like shield, harmless and pleasantly warm. Laughing at their expressions, I tossed the orb into the air. "Catch!"

They didn't even have time to scream.

Sauntering over to their bodies, I knelt down. There wasn't much in the way of remains, so I couldn't close their eyes or anything. "Sorry, boys," I murmured. Rising again, I went back to my examination of the desk which they had indicated might be where the stone was kept.

My movements were hurried now as I waited tensely for the next set of Sayta to come. I wasn't disappointed. Within minutes there were cries of exclamation and horror from outside the burned door. Most of the office had been destroyed, charred beyond recognition. What a waste.

Beyond the remains of the door three Sayta milled, stunned by the wreckage and, no doubt, the amount of power that had radiated from this room a moment ago. I recognized only one of them from the gray stone plain. "Where are Scott and Court?" I yelled, leaving the room for the entrance hall.

They didn't answer. What followed was a massive series of attacks that, unfortunately, drained a lot of my energy and power. By the time two Sayta were dead and the last was held captive, my knees were a little shaky. I couldn't give up, of course. I would have to draw on reserves of strength, fighting onward. The thought made me snort. It sounded like it came out of some romance action/adventure novel. I was ashamed for even thinking of it.

I knelt on my captive's stomach, knees digging painfully into the woman's midsection. "Hello, Hannah," I said pleasantly. She whimpered and struggled to escape the bonds of air I had stretched around her. "Ah-ah, none of that," I scolded, tightening the invisible ropes some. She fell silent, staring at me with huge eyes. "Where are Scott and Court?" I asked again. Her lips formed a reply, but no words came out. "Come on, Hannah," I said darkly. "Tell me and I'll kill you painlessly."

Her large eyes were wide with fear. "Upstairs... third room to the left..."

"Not going to beg for mercy?" I asked.

She shivered, and I almost felt a pang of remorse. Almost. But I was too angry at the Sayta to feel sorry for them.

"No," she whispered. She calmed suddenly, her body going limp. "If you don't kill me, Master Court will. And that death will be far worse than anything you could imagine." She smiled serenely. "I may be a Sayta, but that does not mean death by a Rytra is worse than death by an angry Sayta." Her eyes scanned my face, her smooth forehead creasing a little. "Of course, you're not exactly a normal Rytra, are you? You're half and half." She shook her head. "Never thought it possible..."

"Yeah, me neither."

Then she did something unexpected. She smiled. "Your eyes... they aren't the same either. One blue, one brown. Coincidence, I wonder?"

I let go of all the bonds except for the ones on her hands.

"No, somehow I don't think so either. Goodbye, Hannah." Raising a hand in farewell, I let the power stream through my body, giving the death sentence to the waiting elements. She didn't move, didn't convulse. Her eyes were closed, her expression content. I had not thought it possible for a Sayta to want death. But Hannah had proven that they are, indeed, human, and as varied as the rest of us. Looking at the body with pity, I murmured, "I hope you find peace, Hannah."

Turning away, I started up the staircase. It was time to find Court and make him pay for what he had done. I followed Hannah's instructions until I reached the afore-mentioned door.

Not pausing, I pushed it open, raising a shield as I did. No blasts met me, however. Nothing but a hazy feeling of Dark, that is. I fully entered the room, immediately spotting the two men inside. Scott was standing by the window, tense and ready to either fight or flee. In one hand he held the pocket watch. The way he looked at me, with a slightly feral gleam in his eye, told me just how far he had come from the Scott I knew. Before he had always been relaxed in my presence, even when we were fighting. Now, on the other hand, he seemed afraid. I can't truthfully say I didn't feel a smattering of satisfaction.

Court, as opposed to Scott, was sitting in the single chair in the room. His arms were looped lazily over the back of it, and he slumped in a position of complete comfort and surety. That puzzled me... until I saw his eyes. They were wide and gleaming with an insane light, even the milky white one. He wasn't afraid of me simply because he had lost all common sense. It seemed my fire had hurt him in more ways than one. His hands were bandaged, but his mind had also been shattered. I guess my anger, my single-minded purpose to destroy him, had somehow managed to touch his mind. It was now a wasteland, nothing with any worth. With his sanity gone, however, gone also was his fear of me (if he had any to begin with that is). He was now all the more dangerous, simply because he did not think about being cautious, reserving his strength, anymore.

"Long time no see," I said warily, keeping my eyes on Court. If Scott dared attack me, I would sense him.

Court grinned lazily at me, leaning his head back so his white hair brushed the chair. "Indeed," he agreed amiably. He gestured towards the bed. "Won't you have a seat?"

"I'd rather stand, thanks."

"Really? That's too bad. It would have been so much easier for Scott to attack if you were sitting."

My eyes widened. I turned; power blazing, finally facing Scott instead of the insane Sayta in the chair. Surely he can't be such a fool! I screamed silently.

Scott looked at me blankly, his grayish eyes glittering with amusement. Behind me, Court began to chuckle. "You truly are a fool, Josephine Whitwalker," he hissed.

Darkness and fire melded together, a deadly weapon to anybody, rushed forward, hitting me squarely in the back before I could get my shield strong enough to deflect it.

Stupid, stupid, stupid. How could I fall for such a simple-minded trick? I cannot give a competent answer, simply because I do not wish to make an excuse for my foolishness. Maybe I had been too tense. I had been expecting an attack, of course. How could I not have been? Maybe I was so wary of the upcoming attack, and when I heard that Scott was going to try and kill me, I reacted before my common sense could warn me.

The power hit me heavily, knocking me to my knees, then my stomach. All the air was blown out of my body painfully, leaving me gasping like a stranded fish. Through the haze of pain, I was dimly surprised and pleased that I was still alive. I was dazed, and merely lay there limply for a few seconds, struggling to regain my senses. By the time I had, however, someone was grabbing me, hoisting me up. Coughing, gagging on the bitter, metallic taste of blood in my mouth, I stared at Scott. Bringing up my fist too quickly for him to react, I pegged him right on the jaw, hurling him backwards a few steps, right into a standing lamp. It crashed heavily to the floor, sending shards of glass skittering everywhere. I backed carefully away from him. He glared at me, but didn't make another move. He was either too wary, or too scared, or both.

Keeping the corner of my eye on him, I turned toward Court. He had risen from his chair, and was facing me with a silly, loose grin on his face. "You survived," he drawled heavily. He took a step forward, tripped on nothing, and staggered in an effort to retain his balance.

"Surprised?" I gave him a disgusted look. "You seem to be drunk."

He didn't reply to the last comment. "Yes, as a matter of fact, I am," he answered. "Most people would be long dead."

"Yeah, well, I'm not most people. You're forgetting, Court, that I'm Sayta now. I can withstand some things."

"Some things," he agreed. "But not all. I can kill you, Whitwalker, and I will."

Fire and earth, woven together. Reflected by a thick shadow shield. A burst of light, swallowed by darkness. Raging darkness and earth, melding together, dissipated by water and light. An attack on the other side! Sudden, but weak. Easily defended against, easily destroyed and countered. Scott grunted as he failed to bring up a shield in time, falling under the heavy blow. Blood ran down the side of his face, falling in rivulets down the lines in his cheeks. He wiped it away with his sleeve, glaring at me as he fought back to his feet. With a disdainful glance, I jerked my hand upwards quickly. The earth followed the movement coming up under Scott's feet and throwing him into the air. Fingers splayed, I wound the earth around him as a cocoon. He fought angrily, and I gasped with surprise as he nearly managed to free himself.

The feel of sharp metal-like darkness that burned like fire biting into my skin made me twirl, gasping in pain. I raised a hand, feeling the warm blood drip slowly down my side. Holding the wound tightly, I started to let the healing water flow through me into the nasty gash. Court holding a heavy, two-handed sword changed my mind. With a yell, I ducked the downwards swing, darting as quickly as I could behind him. He turned unexpectedly fast, his sword coming up to my face. I threw myself backwards, half my mind on the sword and half on the still-struggling figure of Scott.

That strange, exhilarating but frightening anger was back, replacing any cold shield I might have had. A growl rose up in my throat as I pushed myself up to my feet, forming my own weapon out of fire, light, and darkness all together. Two slightly curved swords appeared, shimmering with magic. I grabbed onto the smooth, copper-bound hilts. The substance was warm on my palms, sending a thrill through me. I shivered slightly, locking eyes with Court.

When Emily had died, I had promised myself to learn the art of swordsmanship. I wasn't good, but I knew some things. I had been caught unprepared that day; I wouldn't be on this one.

Two steps forward, right sword up, left sword swinging to the side. My opponent twisted away from one, blocking the other with his great blade. The clash from the two blades meeting sent a jolt up my arm, making me wince. It might not have been so bad if I had been fresh into the fight, but my strength was already quickly fading. I had fought too much that day, expended too much power. Scott, hanging in the air on a pillar of earth, was diverting a flow of my power, also. He would just not give up, despite the fact that he surely must be tiring as well. I couldn't stop, though. Stopping was completely out of the question.

Blood pooled beneath my feet, making the floor treacherous, drenching my pant legs. The smell of it filled my nose, sharp in the back of my throat. My wound was making me weaker, draining me of energy as my lifeblood seeped onto the floor. The sharp stabs of pain were enough to make me waver. But I went on. Sidestepping his parry, I brought both swords inward. Once again he managed to dodge one, but the other cut deeply into his cheek. Jumping back a step, I brought both swords into an X in front of me, neatly catching the descending sword. Muscles straining, I pushed him away hard enough to make him stagger.

He retaliated quickly enough, bringing the great two-handed sword down. I dodged, and it bit into the floor with a sickeningly loud crack. With strength that surprised me, Court immediately brought the sword back up, groaning only slightly, and attempted another swing. Backing up, I stepped on something that crunched loudly: the remains of the lamp. I kicked them out of the way, the glass from the bulb skittering loudly around the floor.

I stepped close to Court now, forcing my tiring arms up. The swords, acting almost of their own free will, collided with Court's. His sword dipped to the ground from the clash and the other arm went out wide. I darted into the opening without hesitation. My right sword plunged into his chest deeply. Dark blood spurted in a fountain, drenching us both. His eyes wide, Court froze, body trembling but standing still. His suddenly sightless eyes searched the room widely, finally recognizing and locking onto my face. His eyes were wild, filled with insanity. Then he grinned. Blood lined his lips, trickling down the sides of his mouth. Something about that grin made a tendril of fear grow in me. Hesitation born of that fear filled me, making me wonder if this man could possibly have something else up his sleeve.

His eyes never leaving mine, Court dipped into his pocket. He slowly withdrew a plain gray stone. I blinked, looking at the stone as he raised it to eye-level. Slowly I backed away, not taking my eyes off Court as I slid the sword out of his chest. It came free with a sucking sound, blood dripped quicker onto the floor. I let the swords disappear, so with a free hand I could reach out and take the stone.

"Ah-ah-ah," he murmured in a scolding tone. "I don't think so."

Smirking, he closed his eyes, one dark, and one milky white, curled his fist around the stone, and gave it the power of fire.

The explosion rocked me off my feet. Scott was screaming, yelling out something incoherent. The magnificent building we were in began to collapse, the stone and wood rumbling and creaking as fire raced along its walls.

So destructive—fire. It burned down Hotel Fairdown, killing my best friend, and now it was ravishing this old building. The warm flames were everywhere, licking my skin, making me scream. Thick, heady smoke clogged the air, choking me, slowly killing me. Above everything, above my screams and Scott's, was laughter. Wild, insane cackling filled the thick air, making me shiver despite the monstrous heat.

Everything added together, from the heat to the wound on my side, made me dizzy. The flames that had burned me had seemed to settle into my skin, pricking sharply but no longer killing. Maybe, because fire was now in my blood, I was immune to it. My Sayta half had finally reacted to it, overcoming the Rytra weakness of fire. It was warm, almost pleasantly so, making me sleepy. Eyelids like sandbags, they slowly slid down, blocking my already-blurry vision. The floor was weak beneath me, but I didn't really notice. Even if that fact had penetrated my brain, I doubt I would have had enough energy to do anything about it. Darkness hovered at the edges of my consciousness, and with a beckoning, overwhelmed me.

I came to suddenly, violently, with the stench of smoke filling my nose. Sitting upright, I groaned deeply. My breathing was too fast and heavy, seeming to tug me down. Casting a glance around the room, I saw the devastating effects of the fire. For the most part, there was no more room. The walls were almost gone, leaving me exposed to the cool air. It was late afternoon: I had been unconscious a long time. Most of the furniture was nearly unrecognizable. It was safe to assume that the rest of the house was in the same condition.

Knowing the state of the house, I dared to look down at myself. It was not a pretty sight. Shivering, I noticed my skin was glowing softly, red in more than one place. When I touched those places, I winced as the dull pain flared up into full-blown aching and throbbing. My side was in horrid condition. Blood had congealed around the wound, partially covering it. Every movement brought another stab of horrendous pain. Gasping, eyes watering, I reached up to hold my poor side as I struggled to my feet.

A few paces away, white strands on a charred body told me the fate of Court. Forcing back my disgust, I edged forward, nudging the ashes with the toe of my barely intact boot. There, near what I assumed was his hand, a few pieces of stone remained. No power emanated from it.

The gray stone had finally been destroyed, never again to be a threat to Rytra.

The pocket watch! I thought with a burst of panic. I

spun, too quickly in my weakened state. With another moan, I fell jarringly to my knees. I forced myself back up, pushing the pain far away. There, right before me, was the pillar of earth I had made to contain Scott. It was amazing I hadn't noticed it before. Stumbling over to it, I put a hand on the hard earth. It was warm on my palm, even after all this time had passed. Wavering on my feet, I dispelled the element. The pain sent me to my knees. I barely had any power left when I woke up, and now it was gone altogether. It would be days before I could summon an element again. If Scott had somehow managed to stay alive, then I was doomed.

The earth crumbled away and a dark red body fell to the ground. A cry of horror escaped my lips before I could stop it. Scott's sightless eyes stared up at me, his mouth stretched wide with terror. He had been baked alive in my restraints of earth when Court turned the room into an inferno. His last restraint had become a kiln.

Letting my weak knees take over, I slumped to the ground beside the body. Hands trembling wildly with overexertion and pain, I reached out and began to search my former co-worker.

In his front left pocket, my hand closed on something warm, round, and completely intact. I pulled out the pocket watch. It wasn't even charred. Something to do with the magic inside it, no doubt.

Clutching the artifact close to my heart, I began to cry.

TWENTY

Closing Curtain

I stood at the bedside of Nathanial. He was the same, still deathly ill but in a coma. In one hand I held the golden pocket watch tightly; as if afraid I would lose it.

"Are you sure you should be doing this?" Amy asked anxiously. "You're not fully recovered, after all."

"I know," I replied simply, never taking my eyes off the face of the man I loved. "But I have to do this now."

She sighed in agreement and moved out of the room, closing the door behind her. Alone once more, I carefully knelt, wincing as the wound in my side was pulled taut.

Dyose had been the one to find me. Once he learned where I had gone, he went to the house in the woods immediately—and found me the lone survivor. Naturally, he wasn't too pleased with me, and the tension between us was heavy. I wasn't sure if he would ever forgive me for what I had done... or ever have any trust in me again, now that I could control the Dark as well.

But other things were well. For by defeating Scott and Court, by using the Dark but never losing sight of the Light, I had banished my nightmares. My demons. I could breathe again.

Taking in a deep, slightly shaky breath, I reached out to

place my hands lightly on Nathanial's wounded chest. With the pocket watch held between my domed palms, I closed my eyes and concentrated, reaching deep inside to the very reserves of my strength. Drawing them up, I called to the water and began the process of healing.

After what felt like forever, I drew away. Panting and shaking, I clutched my hands to my chest in an effort to still them. The pocket watch had greatly increased my power, but it seemed like all my power was gone once more. I had never healed so much before, nor so strongly. It was both terrifying and wildly satisfying. I now knew why some Rytra devoted their whole life to healing. Color had risen in Nathanial's cheeks, and his breathing was normal. I was confident that I had purged every ounce of darkness from his body and soul, leaving him clean and pure once more. Despite this, he still might not wake up. The Dark of the Sayta might have sunk into him too much to keep him alive. But there was still hope, like a bright little flame in the center of my heart.

"Please," I whispered. "Please, wake up. Don't let me have been too late."

As if in response to my words, his eyelashes fluttered. Not even daring to breathe, I waited in suspense. A groan escaped his lips, and his eyes slowly opened. The familiar face turned to look at me, blue eyes meeting my own mismatched ones. He blinked slowly.

"Jo?"

His voice was weak, but it was the same deep voice that always sent shivers down my spine. The same voice that made me listen no matter what. The voice that I had grown to long to hear. It seemed ages since I last heard it.

"Yes," I whispered, reaching out to cup his face. I could barely see him through the blur of tears. A broken laugh rose through my throat, thick and shaky from the tears. "Yes. I'm here."

He seemed amazed. Reaching out, he wiped away the tears that flowed down my face. He drew me close, his body warm against mine. "How?" he whispered into my hair. One hand combed through my short locks, while the other tightly gripped by back and waist as if afraid that if he let me go, I would never return. "I thought I died."

"No," I whispered into his chest. "You're alive. We're alive."

He laughed and held me close. "Do you know what I was thinking of when I went over the cliff?" He didn't wait for me to answer, but plowed ruthlessly on. "All I could think of was how much I loved you."

I drew away slowly, staring at him with wide eyes. He watched me with a slight smile on his lips, which grew when he saw my expression.

Then, quite before I could stop myself, I blurted out, "I love you, Nathanial."

He laughed outright at that, eyes crinkling pleasantly. "That's good," he murmured as he leaned forward a bit. "I wouldn't know what to do otherwise."

Then he kissed me, and everything in the world was perfectly and utterly right.

The funeral took place a week later. It was in Ireland, Ian's native land and the place he loved best. It was green every-where as only Ireland can be, from the grass dotted with brown graves to the large trees overshadowing the cemetery. Despite this, one could not shake off the feeling of darkness and death that overhung the partly cloudy day.

Because Ian's body had been completely burned by the fire, there was no filled casket. Instead, a coffer held hand-fuls of ashes taken from Hotel Fairdown in the area I had last seen him standing in my vision. Nathanial and I had gone back to gather the ashes—it was the only thing we could do. Flowers were all around it, partially covering the beautifully carved box. The coffer was set on a raised bier, ready to go into the square deep hole already prepared for it in the McKinley family plot.

Ian's whole village seemed to have gathered around the tent that covered the grave site. The wind was cold and chilling. More than one person openly wept, the women holding handkerchiefs to their eyes, the men bowing their heads in an effort to hide the wetness. The preacher in his black robes spoke solemnly, his Irish accent thick, and his words hung in the air, lingering over our heads.

Nearby, Mum cried into Davy's shoulder. Dyose was there as well, although he made sure to stay away from me. Other Rytra had gathered, but the sad affair didn't stop them from sending me little glances, some merely curious, most at least a little hostile. I didn't try to convince them that this was what had to happen, in order for the stone to be destroyed. They wouldn't understand, and I didn't expect them to.

The pastor finished his speech, motioning for me to come up. Swallowing hard, I barely felt the reassuring squeeze Nathanial gave my hand. Wiping my streaming eyes, I went up to the coffer, laying one hand on its carved top. Turning to face the crowd gathered to see off their dear friend, I was briefly at a loss for words. I hadn't written a speech beforehand, preferring the words to just flow. Working moisture back into my mouth, I began to speak. The words flowed from my tongue, barely processed in my brain before coming out of my mouth.

"All of you gathered here today are to see off a very dear man: Ian McKinley. He was my best friend. He was always there for me, no matter what. I'm sure all of you know of his bravery, his loyalty, and his good nature. Wherever he was, the room seemed just a little bit brighter." Tears pricked my eyes, and I didn't bother to stem them. What was the point of that? I would just break down again a minute later. "Now, however, he's gone from us." Sobs rose from the crowd, swarming around me like a thick blanket. "Despite this, that room will never dim. While he may not be here physically, Ian will live on in our spirits, in our hearts, and in our memories."

I managed to swallow my tears. "A wise man, George S. Patton, Jr., once said 'It is foolish and wrong to mourn the men who died. Rather we should thank God that such men lived.' And I do thank God every day that I was privileged to have him in my life. Let us honor what I believe his wishes are and keep him alive in our hearts forever."

Taking a single flower from the bouquets of lilies I had

brought, I set it on top of the coffer. It wavered there in the wind, the white petals bright against the dark wood. Men moved forward and began to lower the coffer into the ground. The flowers were set aside, waiting to be put on top of the grave. All except for the single lily. Fresh dirt was piled on, covering the box. Most people waited only until the dirt was firmly packed in before leaving. They passed by me, putting a hand on my shoulder, whispering condolences in my ear. I heard none of them. All I heard was Ian's voice, whispering he loved me. All I saw was his countenance, his laughing smile. That was all that mattered.

At last, everyone except Nathanial and I had left. The headstone at the top of the grave was standard gray marble, with the Celtic cross on top. Across the front was engraved:

Ian McKinley
1985-2007
Dear Son and Friend
~Rest in Peace~

My tears were all spent, so it was dry-eyed that I knelt by the freshly turned earth and murmured, "Goodbye, old friend. I'll miss you. At least… at least now you can meet Emily. You can keep each other company until I join you."

Rising, I turned and walked over to Nathanial. He was waiting a few paces away, letting me have a last moment alone with Ian. I gratefully leaned into him.

"You okay?" he asked me.

I nodded slowly. "I'm not perfect, but I'm healing—slowly but surely."

Nathanial made a small noise of agreement. Silence settled over us for a while, broken only by the soft rustling of trees. At last Nathanial spoke again. "What now?"

I looked down at my hands. "We go forward," I answered slowly. "We go forward into the future and try to live the best we can."

"Jo," Nathanial berated gently. "Can't you do any better?"

The chastisement didn't bother me in the least. In fact, I gave him a small smile. "All right, how about this? We stay here until you're fully recovered and everything's fine again, and then we go back to Seattle."

Nathanial's eyebrows rose.

"I know," I agreed. "But Ian left me his house. I have to do something with it."

We had mutually agreed that Nathanial would quit RODD in Seattle. I knew I could never again be accepted in most RODD circles, if any. Dyose didn't want me in Seattle, and I was perfectly fine with having a two-person RODD of my own. "Once we're settled wherever, we will do what we always have done—fight Sayta."

He smiled, but it faded after a moment. "It'll be hard, Jo," he warned. "Not belonging to RODD, and being hunted by Sayta and Rytra, most likely."

While most Rytra would probably leave me alone, even if they would never help me again, I'm sure there are some out there that would like nothing better than to kill me because of the Sayta powers streaming through my blood. And the Sayta... well, I was still Rytra, and they wouldn't ever consider letting me live. But I had faced the Dark once; I could—I would—do it again.

"I know," I murmured softly. "It's a thin line to walk—the line between good and evil." I turned back to Nathanial, smiling once more. "But I have a feeling I'll be fine. We'll be fine. After all, I'm the person who restored the balance between Rytra and Sayta, at least for the moment, so I seem to have some agility."

"Humph," he snorted slightly as I stumbled over a rock in the path. But his eyes gleamed with amusement and love.

"And besides," I said, gripping his hand tighter, "should I lose my balance and fall, I have you to catch me."